ALPHA SQUAD

Showdown

LORELEI MOONE

eXplicitTales

Copyright © 2017 Lorelei Moone,
Cover art by Silver Heart Publishing
Published by eXplicitTales
All rights reserved.
ISBN-13: 9781913930264

CONTENTS

PROLOGUE

<hr>

"Relax, it won't hurt a bit," Erin said.

Although he still looked uncertain, the young guy who'd taken a seat in the chair beside her did hold out his arm.

"I just don't like needles."

"I totally understand. But it's all for a good cause, right?" Erin asked.

Small talk didn't normally come easily to her, but right now was an exception. After weeks of drudgery, she was in her element.

This blood donation drive was the single best thing that had happened during her entire time at the lab. Finally, she was allowed to do a whole lot more than data entry and other dumb stuff that probably should have been outsourced to robots by now.

Erin scanned the clinic which was normally only accessible by those people participating in one of the various medical trials the university sponsored.

Professor Blake was thankfully far out of sight, allowing her some more leeway with this reluctant donor.

"What's your name?" Erin asked.

"Jeremy."

"I promise, I'll be gentle." She smiled as she unsealed a

fresh donation kit.

Jeremy forced a smile, but kept eyeing her hands as the needle neared his arm.

Right then, something weird happened. It was as though his arm changed color just for a second.

"Whoa!" Erin said, pulling her hand back. Had she just imagined that?

She looked at Jeremy, who seemed even more flustered now.

"I'm sorry. Please carry on," he mumbled.

"What was that?" she whispered, unaware that she'd voiced her question out loud.

"Really. It won't happen again. I've got it under control."

Erin frowned. So she hadn't imagined it.

"You're..." she mumbled. "You're one of *them*!"

"A shifter. Yes."

Erin quickly covered her mouth with her free hand. "I'm sorry, that came out wrong."

"No problem. I can see how that would freak you out. Seriously though, I'm okay now," Jeremy said.

Erin's heart rate about doubled in speed and intensity. She raised her hand again, and found that her fingers were trembling. But it wasn't fear that she felt. It was excitement.

She took a deep breath. *Focus, woman! It isn't every day that you get to take a shifter's blood! Don't mess it up!*

"So, what's it like? Being able to change what you look

like at will?" she mumbled. "It seems really cool."

Jeremy's eyes met hers as he looked up at her in surprise, giving her the chance to get the needle in swiftly.

"Oh!" he exclaimed. "You're right, that wasn't so bad." He looked down at the deep red liquid filling the clear tube attached to his arm. It didn't take long for the blood bag to start filling up. The rate at which the blood flowed from Jeremy's arm was quicker than Erin had come to expect.

"It was a serious question, though. What's it like?" she whispered.

Jeremy grinned. "A lot better now that I don't have to hide it anymore."

"I bet," she said.

Erin had to force herself to stop staring at the guy, who looked like he was in his late teens.

He must be a student here, she thought. *I wonder how many more there are?*

Erin scanned the other chairs dotted throughout the clinic. That was when she caught a glimpse of Professor Blake from the corner of her eye. So much for the peace and quiet she'd enjoyed so far. Meanwhile, the bag attached to Jeremy's arm had filled up completely.

"Alright. Looks like we're all done here," she said as she fastened a dressing around his arm. "It's important that you take it easy for a little bit. And help yourself to the snacks. Any faintness you may feel will pass soon enough, but please let someone know if you're starting to feel unwell."

"I'm fine, really."

"At least have a pastry and a cold drink or something," Erin urged.

"If you insist. Thanks. This wasn't bad at all."

"Cool, well…" Erin glanced up to find the professor gesturing at his watch with a grim expression on his face. He was a lot of things, but kind or patient weren't part of the list.

"I hope to see you at the next donation camp!" Erin said.

Jeremy waved as he got up and walked straight towards the refreshments table. Before she had the chance to process what had just happened, another donor sat down in front of her.

Erin safely put away the bag with Jeremy's donation, disposed of the needle, and squeezed some antiseptic gel into her hand.

"Hi there. Please let me examine your arm for a suitable spot," Erin said, almost on autopilot. Her encounter with Jeremy the shifter was too significant to just let go like that.

Although it was unlikely she'd come across him on her way to and from work—Professor Blake's lab was in a different campus from where most classes were held— Erin hoped she'd see him again. She had so many questions.

She stole a glance at him as he was leaving, marveling at

the smoothness of his movements. The differences were subtle, but he didn't walk like a normal person, did he?

How she'd love to find out more about him and his kind. How she'd love to study someone like him if given half the chance. Not in a creepy, lock-'em-up-and-stick-needles-in-'em kind of way, but just to *understand*. Okay, perhaps there'd be some needles, just for the occasional sample.

Someone loudly cleared his throat right behind her, making Erin flinch.

Professor Blake.

She shivered slightly, but then regained her composure. *Back to work! These donors aren't going to drain themselves!*

CHAPTER ONE

Joining Alpha Squad was never meant to be easy.

Sean McMillan rested both hands on the wash basin, with his eyes fixed straight ahead at the mirror. He wasn't looking at himself as such, just staring through his reflection at nothing.

Bentley—the gruff former SAS man responsible for his training—had warned him before he'd started boot camp; the others on the squad had joked and teased him about the same.

But the intense training he'd undergone hadn't bothered him. He'd welcomed the physical and mental challenges. And anyway, training was over now. He'd survived.

What ate at him this morning—most mornings, actually—went much deeper.

Had he made the right choice?

His career on the Kent police force had been on an upward trajectory. At just under thirty, he'd made detective. He'd enjoyed the work and was good at it.

And ever since the string of murders near the Sevenoaks shifter refugee camp had been solved, things had gone a little nuts. He'd been singled out as somewhat of a hero and been given his pick of cases and assignments.

And yet, he'd left everything behind to join Alpha Squad.

Justifications for this decision were easy to sum up; the chance to do something different; to make a difference on a national scale; to be a part of a new agency which enjoyed the support of an entire government ministry. Still, none of that rang true; Sean could not explain to himself why he was really here.

He did not belong.

This wasn't a new feeling, of course. He'd always carried with him a sense that he was different somehow even when he was young. When he hit puberty, his dad had taken him aside and explained a few things about what it meant to be a shifter. About the importance of getting his urges under control. To keep his nature a secret at all costs.

He was already taller and stronger than most boys his age, so nobody really messed with him. But he didn't have a lot of friends in secondary school either. Not that that bothered him.

Sean had always been quite content in his own company. He preferred listening to talking, something that would serve him well in his professional life so far.

What he found hard to accept was that there was this whole other side to him which he was just meant to ignore. He'd gotten over it though. And now he was facing the other side of that dilemma.

Here he was, part of a brave new world where shifters no longer needed to hide. That dirty little secret he'd carried with him all his life was no longer a secret. The team consisted of more shifters than humans, and they didn't shy away from showing off their peculiar transformational talents should the situation demand it. Even if it didn't. It was like it was all a big game to them.

That was the biggest shock he'd faced upon arriving on base. It wasn't uncommon for one or more of the team to spontaneously morph into their animal selves to go out for a run around the woods. No matter how often they'd encouraged him to join in, Sean had been unable to bring himself to. It simply felt *wrong* to let his animal side out.

He forced himself to snap out of his pointless thoughts by splashing cold water on his face. Onwards and upwards. He'd chosen to be a part of the squad, so he wouldn't allow himself to give up so easily. Perhaps once he went on his first mission, all these doubts would fade.

———◆———

"First of all, congratulations to Sean McMillan, who is officially a full member of the squad as of today," Major Williams began her briefing.

Sean felt everyone's eyes on him. He should be proud of this achievement, but he still had some doubts about the entire affair.

"Good job, mate," Benjamin Cooper, one of the two

humans on the team, told him.

Sean nodded.

Out of everyone on the team, he could relate to Cooper the best. Bentley, of course, was too abrasive and distant. And the shifters… well, they were shifters. Cooper was simple. A man like so many others Sean had come across in his previous job.

"Now, I'm afraid there's no time to relax or celebrate. We have a mission," the major continued.

"Aw, man!" Cooper complained under his breath.

It wasn't loud enough for the major to hear, but Sean could. Eric King, who stood next to the major, did shoot a disapproving look in his direction. Obviously Cooper—who'd spent months on the team already—had not yet grown accustomed to the shifters' extra sensitive hearing picking up on just about everything he chose to utter, no matter how quietly.

"This case is different," Major Williams said. "In the sense that we weren't called in by the local authorities. They don't even know we're coming. And until we find some tangible proof of foul play, it's probably best that they don't find out. We don't wish to step on anyone's toes."

Eric King stepped up next to Major Williams and cleared his throat.

"For this reason we'll be going in undercover," he said.

Sean frowned. He was on the other side now. No

longer part of local law enforcement, but a full-fledged member of Alpha Squad. It was obvious that they'd play by their own rules. But a part of him still disapproved of their idea to deceive local police. Of course, he kept his concerns to himself.

"Private Callahan, if you don't mind distributing the name badges and uniforms," Major Williams interjected.

"Nice one! I hope I get to have a cool name and cover story!" Cooper quipped.

Bentley sighed and rolled his eyes at the younger man.

Nobody else commented. Adam King, Eric's brother and youngest squad member, accepted his ID in silence. Next up, Private Callahan reached Cooper.

"Aw damn. I'm just me!" he complained.

Sean received his badge to find the same thing. Good. Fewer lies to remember.

He studied the rest of the badge. University of the Highlands and Islands. They were going to Scotland?

Sean's father had been from Scotland, though he'd never talked about his family or where he grew up, so Sean didn't know where his roots lay exactly.

"And what is it we're investigating?" Sean looked up from his badge as soon as he'd completed the question.

"We're not entirely sure," Eric said. "I've received a call from an old friend who lives up there. It seems there have been some suspicious deaths within the shifter community in Inverness." Major Williams cleared her throat. "Both victims had connections to the local university, so that's where we'll focus our energy."

"And the local police aren't investigating these deaths?" Sean questioned.

"The medical examiner has ruled the deaths as natural causes. Heart failure," Major Williams explained.

Sean frowned again. If the bodies have been examined properly, and there was nothing suspicious about them, then what was the squad meant to investigate, exactly? It was fairly common for survivors to see foul play where there was none, simply because they didn't want to accept that a loved one had died. He'd dealt with that kind of thing more than once in his old job. Perhaps that was what had inspired Eric's friend to call in the squad.

"I hate to be skeptical," Sean began, "But if the medical examiner—an expert in his or her field—is satisfied that these unfortunate people died of natural causes, why are we looking to challenge that?"

"That's pretty obvious," Adam King answered without giving his brother a chance to. "Shifters don't just get heart attacks."

"That's right," Eric confirmed.

Damn. Sean pressed his lips together. He really should have known that. Sadly, his police training hadn't come with a handbook on peculiar facts about shifters. Bentley hadn't covered this sort of stuff in his Alpha Squad training either. They probably assumed he knew everything already…

"That leaves two possibilities," Thomas Blackwood, the only wolf on the squad, remarked. "Murder or suicide."

"Suicide? Really?" Adam said.

"It's worth mentioning both options," Blackwood said and folded his arms.

This . This right here was why Sean's transition into the team had been a struggle. He was used to knowing his stuff. To feeling capable and in control. Here it was like he didn't know jack shit and it was getting on his nerves.

Sean had more questions, of course, but he kept them to himself. Making a fool of himself once today was enough.

"Cooper and McMillan," Eric spoke up again. "We've arranged for you to join the university as security guards, which will give you access to most of the campus. Adam, as the youngest team member, you'll pose as a student and attempt to find out about the victim's social life and movements during the final moments before his death. I'll accompany you, but the rest of the squad will sit this one out. We don't want to attract so much attention."

Fine . Sean was relieved that he was being paired with Cooper and not one of the other guys. The man wasn't overly clever, but he was at least predictable.

Perhaps once they got out into the field, he would find his way out of this funk and feel useful again. After all, an investigation like this was exactly the sort of thing he was good at. Sort of. Minus the shifter angle, obviously.

Plus, how hard could it be to pretend to be a security

guard? This wasn't his first undercover gig.

Sean remained silent throughout the rest of the briefing and just tried to listen. Two dead shifters. Heart failure that couldn't have been natural. One of the victims had been a current student at the university, the other an alumnus. Other than the fact they were both shifters, the university was the only obvious connection between them.

If he was running this investigation, he would have probably set things up in a very similar fashion, though he might have preferred to involve the local authorities first. The university campus was the logical starting point for their enquiries. All the better that they were able to insert Adam as a student. Campus security wasn't as intimidating as regular police, but a uniform was a uniform. Students would still feel awkward opening up to McMillan or Cooper.

Major Williams ended the briefing, giving them all a chance to pack up their things. They'd move out two hours later. Sean waited until the rest of the squad had left, before approaching the major for a quiet word.

"I'd love to take a look at the file if that's okay," he said, gesturing at the papers Major Williams had referred to during the briefing.

She nodded. "Here you go. Glad to have you on the team, McMillan. Your experience makes you a valuable addition to the squad."

Sean nodded. "Thank you, Ma'am."

He hoped she was right. As far as he was concerned, this mission was make or break for him. Either he'd be able to contribute and help solve the case, or he really had no business being here at all.

Back in his quarters, Sean took about ten minutes to deposit his most essential belongings into an overnight bag. The rest of the time he spent poring over what little facts the squad had received about the two victims. He memorized the facts, as he normally did when he got a new case. He found that cramming every last detail into his mind helped him make connections, often subconsciously, as he discovered new evidence.

He might have learned a whole bunch of new things during boot camp, but that was no reason to change what had worked for him in his previous job.

By the time they headed to the local train station, he felt as ready as he was going to be.

CHAPTER TWO

Change was in the air, Erin could feel it. Today was the day that would turn everything around.

After the obligatory large cup of tea and two Hobnobs she usually enjoyed for breakfast, she headed to the lab, filled with a sense of optimism which she hadn't felt ever since starting this godawful job.

The weather was ordinary. The sun had a hard time breaking through the clouds that seemed ever-present in this part of Scotland.

Inverness was not known for its hot summers.

The work was monotonous as ever, though. A breakthrough seemed completely out of reach.

Working for one of the leading geneticists in the country had sounded exciting enough; a participant in the now concluded Human Genome Project, Professor Blake was a man at the forefront of his field. Or so she'd heard.

The reality on ground in the lab was far from interesting, though.

Rather than assisting in his research, and learning from the man, Erin's job had mostly involved making copious cups of tea, managing the professor's calendar, or any number of menial tasks around the lab which none of her colleagues wanted to do. The work was duller than stacking shelves at the local supermarket. Erin would know. That was what she'd done part time to put herself through university.

At least there, taking initiative was somewhat encouraged...

Sadly, this had been the only opening in Erin's field within hundreds of miles. Until she managed to get more experience, she didn't have the luxury of other options.

There's got to be a better use of my time, Erin wondered, as she prepared dozens of slides for inspection, dripping exactly one drop of blood from each sample onto each slide and labelling it with the correct serial number. She had no concrete idea what the samples were or what Blake was looking for exactly, though she did have a few theories. While processing a previous batch of samples, she'd taken a peek at some of them under an old fashioned microscope she'd found in one of the storage cupboards.

Those particular samples had definitely been human.

And there were always two dozen of them.

Whatever Blake was working on, Erin imagined it must be very important. Some big question the scientific community hadn't been able to answer so far. Blake was obviously planning on figuring things out on his own, and taking sole credit when the time came to publish his findings. Why else would he guard his research so carefully?

It hadn't taken long for the hopeful mood Erin had woken up with to evaporate. Even with her earphones in and the volume on her phone cranked up high, she couldn't find peace.

There was no progress to be found here. As usual.

And still, sometime after mid-morning, in the midst of transcribing page after page of data Professor Blake had left for her, Erin felt another flutter of excitement come over her. It certainly wasn't sparked by anything she was up to in the lab, but seemed to originate deep inside her.

She couldn't explain it. Neither could she bear to sit still.

Erin dumped Blake's handwritten notes into a drawer underneath her desk, then switched off the music.

"I'm going out for a breath of fresh air," Erin announced as she stuck her head around the doorway leading to the only other person inside the lab's workstation.

Glenn barely looked up from his work, just muttered something unintelligible. Erin shrugged. She hadn't known Professor Blake's only other assistant to be chatty, ever, so his reaction was as expected.

On her way out, she did not look back. It was like her feet had a mind of their own, spurring her on to go faster and faster until she was almost ready to break into a jog by the time she reached the glass-clad reception area of the university campus.

Erin suddenly stopped, not by choice, really, but by instinct, as her gaze rested on a small group of uniformed men who'd just entered the atrium.

She recognized one of them—Mel, the guard who she'd exchanged the odd pleasantry with during those lonely evening shifts when the rest of the campus was basically abandoned. The others were new.

One in particular caught her eye. Tall, with a full head of dark blond hair, and shoulders broad enough to carry the world on them.

Turn around, will you? Erin thought.

He didn't, though, leaving Erin no other option but to desperately stare at his back. A funny sensation had filled her chest. Like she was ready to burst into a million pieces. It was unlike anything she'd felt before, so there was no way she could tear herself away from the scene.

Mel was gesturing as though he was giving them directions. The other man, who was facing in Erin's direction, nodded in agreement. He was fit enough, especially compared to Mel, who was slightly on the heavier side, though he still had nothing on the mystery man who still had his back turned toward her.

Erin still couldn't look away. There was something familiar about that guy. Erin felt an odd sense of déjà-vu. At the same time, she was pretty sure she hadn't seen him before. Both of these guards were new, or she would have remembered them from a previous encounter.

Then what could it be?

Mel waved the two of them along and started to walk in the direction of the double doors leading deeper into the building. As she continued to observe the two new guards walking away, her analytical mind started to work feverishly on the problem in front of her.

Those two didn't just have different builds, they had different walks too. The way the one she'd been staring at moved was fundamentally different. It reminded her of someone... *Jeez, who was it?*

Erin almost forgot to breathe when she connected the dots. The guy at the blood donation camp last week! Jeremy, the shifter!

The similarities between the two were striking, though Jeremy had not been nearly as tall.

Oh my, does that mean this guy's a shifter too?

This possibility made Erin's head spin.

All week she'd been looking out for Jeremy for a chance to ask him more questions. She was desperate to find out more about shifters, from a purely scientific perspective, of course.

And here it was. An opportunity had walked right into Erin's place of work. It was too good to pass up.

This was a sign—it had to be. This was the breakthrough Erin had been waiting for. Fate had something more in store for her. Not that she believed in that sort of thing, but it was the only explanation she had for the strange mood she'd woken up with.

Professor Blake wouldn't approve of her chasing down and questioning people during working hours, but then, he wasn't around today anyway. She'd put in a bit of overtime to finish her pending work. Glenn wouldn't care enough to rat her out; he probably wouldn't even notice what she was up to.

The professor would never know.

Would she dare to approach the shifter?

What would she say to break the ice?

And what the hell was she trying to achieve? Her nosiness had to have a purpose; she needed a plan, or the entire thing would just blow up in her face.

Erin looked down at herself and attempted to fix her slightly wrinkly lab coat with the palm of her hands. At least she already looked the part. And they were here in the Center for Health Sciences, after all. It wouldn't be totally weird to approach someone for a bit of spontaneous research in a place like this, right?

In any case, she couldn't afford to waste any more time.

Erin started to walk, then sped up, breaking into a jog to cross the atrium and catch up with her prospective subject as Mel led him away from her and into the area of the building which was mostly dedicated to diabetes research.

"Umm, excuse me? Hello, Mel!" Erin called out, as she pushed her way through the doors.

The guard stopped and turned. "That's me," he said. "Oh, hey, how can I help you? Erin, is it?"

Erin felt her cheeks redden. The short jog wouldn't have been enough for her to get out of breath normally, but she was severely winded. Nerves. It had to be.

"Actually..." She paused and straightened her back.

Stop being an ass and spit it out already!

"I..." Erin's heartbeat surged as she looked up at the man who'd caught her fancy from afar: strong, symmetrical features and intelligent but kind eyes. He looked to be in his late twenties, just a few years older than she was. The word *handsome* seemed too understated a description, though of course he was.

He was out of this world.

"Yes?" Mel urged.

Erin forced herself to look away from the suspected shifter for a moment in an attempt to organize her thoughts. So instead, she made eye contact with the other, much more normal looking guy. *How am I to be a serious scientist if I can't even speak to my subjects properly?*

"I'm working on a study of sorts... I mean... I was wondering if you'd be willing to answer a few questions to help me out?" she rambled. *Answer questions, perhaps let her take a few blood samples...*

Erin pressed her lips together and tried to focus on her breathing while she waited for a response.

"Hey, hey, I haven't even finished training them yet!" Mel protested.

"During your break, or after your shift, of course," Erin clarified.

"We'll have to check with—" the normal looking man said, until his sentence was cut short by a subtle, yet effective elbow in the ribs from his shifter associate.

"What's this study about, exactly?" the shifter asked.

Erin immediately opened her mouth to answer, but then closed it again.

She'd assumed he was a shifter, based on what exactly? His athletic build and body language? How lame. What if she was mistaken?

Without potentially making a fool of herself, she'd have to take both of the new guards as a package deal. Just as well; it would be good to have a control subject of sorts.

"Oh, you know, the study aims to record patterns in the native Scottish population for various genetic markers, that may or may not be indicators for certain physical traits or health issues—it's rather complicated stuff. Anyway, I'm short a few candidates, so what do you say?" Erin lied.

Mel sighed and impatiently tapped his right foot. "Scientists."

"I'm not Scottish," the human said.

Erin shook her head. "That doesn't matter. You'd be in the control group."

"How would you detect genetic markers by having us answer questions exactly?" the shifter asked.

Busted.

Erin glanced up at the man, whose eyebrows were pulled together in a thoughtful frown, creating a subtle crease just above his nose. He looked even more handsome because of it.

"Okay, you got me. I was hoping to take some blood

samples as well."

"Whoa, okay I don't know if I'm up for that," the other one protested. "I'm not overly keen on getting jabbed with needles unless I absolutely have no other choice!"

"That's fair enough," Erin said. She looked up at the gorgeous shifter again, trying her most convincing pleading look on him.

"I don't know what time we'll finish up today." He gestured at Mel, who now had his arms folded in front of him in an attempt to look stern.

"Why don't you at least take my number," Erin said, while digging around in her pockets for a pen and a piece of paper. The only thing she had on her was an old flyer from the blood donation drive.

She folded it over and scribbled her digits onto the back, then handed it to the shifter. Just like when she'd taken Jeremy's blood a week ago, she noticed that her fingers were trembling ever so slightly.

Bloody nerves.

"Just let me know what you decide," she said, hoping that she sounded rather less desperate than she felt. *I'll be heartbroken if I never see you again.*

The man nodded and put the piece of paper into his pocket without even looking at it. Awkward.

"Okay, I'll let you get on with your work now," Erin mumbled as she made a swift retreat through the double doors. "Thanks for your time!"

As soon as she turned her back and marched back in the direction of Professor Blake's lab, she allowed herself to breathe normally again.

What a guy.

And she'd behaved like a bumbling fool in front of him.

Way to go, she berated herself on her walk back. *No way is he going to call!*

The way she'd been acting, she might have had a better shot if she'd just asked him out for coffee or something. Instead, she'd gone full nerd on the guy and scared him off.

CHAPTER THREE

Sean's initial assessment of the undercover mission had been correct. It wouldn't be too hard to pretend to be a security guard for a bit. The biggest challenge they faced was that Cooper and he had been assigned to the Center for Health Sciences. Although it was a part of the university, it wasn't the main campus.

They were unlikely to learn anything useful about the victim—an eighteen year old wolf shifter named Jeremy Yates—in this place. Chances were he might have never even set foot in here.

Once Mel finished briefing them about the various protocols and security systems, Cooper and he were left to their own devices in the guard's room. After staring at the various surveillance screens for a bit, Cooper broke the silence.

"So, what do you think that woman, Erin, was all about?" he asked.

Something about the way Cooper spoke about her rubbed Sean the wrong way. It was almost as though he felt *protective* of her, which made no sense at all.

Sean shrugged, in an attempt to seem casual, and turned the question around. "I don't know. What do you think?"

Cooper scratched the side of his head. "I'm not sure I

buy the whole research project thing."

Sean frowned. He'd been so distracted during the brief moments spent in Erin's company, he never even analyzed a word she said to him. Was Cooper onto something?

Then again, this was the place where the university's scientific research took place.

"And why is that?"

"Something just doesn't sit right with me. Like how nervous she was."

Sean tried his best to hear his colleague, rather than reject his observations out of hand. This was the first time they were really working together, but previous interactions suggested that the man wasn't particularly observant or sharp. It was possible that his first impressions were wrong.

"Maybe she's awkward around people? Probably spends her days stuck in a lab somewhere," Sean speculated. He couldn't help but wonder where she was and what she was doing right now.

"Yeah, maybe. Or maybe the whole story was just an excuse to talk to us. Maybe she had some ulterior motive."

For a guy who came across as fairly simple and uncomplicated, he seemed to have really thought this through. Sean owed it to Cooper to at least consider the possibility.

"I wonder…"

Sean closed his eyes and tried to relive the whole encounter with Erin, attempting to look at it with an analytical, detective's eye. He failed miserably.

For some strange reason, this woman, Erin, had had a profound effect on him. He'd felt attracted to her from the start, making their conversation awkward to say the least. He'd tried to hide his feelings, and avoided looking at her. Now that he was trying to recall the details of the meeting, it was all a fuzzy mess.

All his mind seemed willing to feed him were glimpses of how her lips moved as she spoke. The way she'd looked up at him when she'd handed him that piece of paper with her phone number. Those big blue eyes, which sought to draw him in. Her beautiful face, framed by fiery red hair and adorned by little freckles...

While he thought of her, it was like he could still catch a whiff of her perfume.

There was a certain innocence and kindness about her; he'd felt it in his heart. Not that *that* observation made any sense.

What the hell was wrong with him? This first mission was supposed to be his chance to redeem himself after feeling like a fish out of water ever since joining the squad. But instead of diving into this investigation in earnest, he'd allowed a random woman to put him off his game.

"McMillan. Oi!" Cooper's voice dragged Sean back to reality.

"What?" Sean swiftly pulled his hand out of his pocket. Without even realizing it, he'd reached for the paper with

Erin's phone number while thinking of her.

"Mate, I don't think you've been listening to me."

Oh? Sean rubbed his eyes and tried to regain focus. "Sorry, Cooper, I think I'm still a bit worn out after all the boot camp training," he lied. It was all that woman. He'd been too busy thinking about her to listen to Cooper.

"Yeah, whatever you say," Cooper mumbled.

"What do you mean?"

"Nothing. It's real boring staring at these screens, that's all. I hope Adam's having more luck over on the main campus."

Finally, something Sean could agree with. They should have been there too. This was starting to look like a waste of time. Or was it?

He held up the folded piece of paper and inspected it more closely. It was thin, almost like tissue paper. He unfolded it and studied her handwriting. A little rushed, but elegant.

Then he turned it over. It wasn't an ordinary piece of note paper, but rather a flyer for some event that had already passed. Why hold onto it?

Sean looked up only to find Cooper already staring at him.

"Find anything?" the latter asked.

"I was just thinking about what you said. That she might have had some other motivation to talk to us. Perhaps we should, you know, look into that possibility."

"Right."

There was something in Cooper's tone that sparked Sean's suspicions.

"What?" he demanded, trying hard not to get annoyed again.

"It just seems like you're a bit keen to talk to her again, you know?"

"No, I don't know. This is what we were sent here to do: investigate."

"Okay, but what are you going to say? Are you going to agree to be her guinea pig for whatever research she's doing?" Cooper asked.

Sean took a deep breath. It would be the most obvious way of getting close to this woman. He shrugged without saying a word.

"I'm not sure the major would be too happy about that," Cooper said.

Sean wasn't even sure he himself was all that happy about it either. Shifters were *out* now, but he still felt awkward about exposing his secret to some random researcher. If she took a sample of his blood to study, would she be able to find out what he was? He simply didn't know. Maybe he shouldn't take the risk at all.

But he couldn't just leave it, could he? He *had* to call her. Even just to prove Cooper wrong.

"I'll work something out that doesn't involve her sticking needles in me. Don't worry," Sean tried to reassure Cooper as much as himself. "Maybe I'll... " *ask her out.*

He couldn't bring himself to say that out loud. Cooper would have a grand time teasing him about it.

And he'd be right to.

Ever since meeting Erin earlier that day, that was the one thing he'd wanted most. He just hadn't been willing to admit it to himself.

"How long 'til end of shift?" Sean asked instead.

Cooper checked his watch. "Another hour or so."

Sean sighed and folded the leaflet with Erin's phone number up again and stuffed it back in his pocket. This was getting ridiculous.

He folded his arms and stared at the screens in front of him again.

"Let's hope Adam's day has been more productive."

"Yep," Cooper agreed.

No matter how much Erin tried stay alert, the rest of the afternoon passed her by in a blur.

That man, the new guard, he'd infiltrated her thoughts like an obsession. Like a disease.

That was, until Professor Blake turned up and started cracking his whip.

"What's going on with these notes, Erin?" he demanded.

She stared sheepishly at the floor. Rather than finish typing up the handwritten papers he had left on her desk, she'd spent much of the afternoon fantasizing about her mystery man. Was he really a shifter? Had she made the right observations?

She really should have asked him out for coffee instead of talking about her stupid non-existent research project. She'd made a huge blunder.

"I'm so sorry, it took me longer than expected to prep the blood samples," Erin said.

Professor Blake didn't want to hear it, and launched straight into a lecture about the importance of a good work ethic, and how many other candidates had applied for Erin's job.

It was no use, though. Erin's mind was still miles away. She nodded and made agreeable noises at the appropriate times during his rant, but she wasn't listening to any of it.

This wasn't the first time Professor Blake had lectured her, and it surely wouldn't be the last. In a way, she was used to it, but today it was especially easy for her to shrug off his tirade. She had way more exciting things to think about, after all.

"I'll stay late and catch up," Erin offered.

Rather than pacify the man, that seemed to set him off more.

"Of course you will! That's the least I would expect!" he shouted.

It took another five minutes or so for him to calm down. Soon, the awkward silence in the lab was broken by the sound of Erin's fingers moving feverishly across the keyboard. If she wanted to get back home at a decent time, she'd better hurry and finish the job.

Professor Blake, meanwhile, got up and walked away. Erin could hear him next door, talking to Glenn in a hushed voice, but she couldn't make out the words. Neither did she care, really.

Her mind was miles away again. That new guard… she'd acted like a fool around him, and no doubt put him off. But perhaps she could still fix that. Maybe if she talked to him again, like a normal human being this time, not a mad scientist…

"Have you finished?" the professor asked as he walked back in.

"Umm…" Erin looked down at the remaining papers.

"You stopped typing."

"The computer was behaving strangely," she said, trying to justify herself.

"Well, seeing as I have your attention, I wanted to let you know that I was hoping to organize another blood donation camp soon."

"Yes? But we've just done one," Erin argued.

"Well, my National Health Service contact and I felt that it went so well, we might as well try again, while there is still—how do you young people say—*buzz* about it. They can never collect too much blood, as you well know."

Erin frowned. There was always a need for more blood

donors, that was true, but she wasn't sure what this supposed *buzz* was that Blake was talking about. It had been hard enough getting people to show up last time.

And since donors are meant to wait eight weeks between donations, they'd have to attract a whole new group of people. It wouldn't be easy.

"I suppose we can approach some local sports teams if they want to help us promote it," Erin suggested. *Or, maybe it would be best to steer the professor in a whole new direction…*

"What about making it not just for blood, but also get people to sign up as organ donors? That way we can try to call back the people who already donated blood the first time around."

Professor Blake nodded, and a subtle smile broke through his otherwise stern face.

"Good thinking. I'm going to leave the marketing side up to you. However you want to handle it. I'm thinking maybe three weeks from now? Have a plan ready tomorrow. And I do still want these notes done by morning."

So much for trying to be helpful. All she managed to achieve was to create more work for herself.

Erin opened her mouth to protest, but then changed her mind. She might as well accept she wasn't getting out of here any time soon.

"Yes, professor," she said instead.

"Wonderful." The professor checked his watch. "I'm

going to be late for a meeting. I trust you'll do the needful."

Erin sighed and nodded.

What was she going to do at home, anyway? Faith, her excitable and overly chatty flat mate, wouldn't be home until after midnight.

So she'd do what, watch TV and order take-out? Perhaps if she hung around here, she might run into that new guard again... *God, wouldn't that be lovely.*

CHAPTER FOUR

By the end of shift, Sean had even more doubts about the whole security guard thing.

He'd been on stake-outs before, which was just about as boring as police work could get. Monitoring campus surveillance systems was worse, though. At least on a stake-out there was a chance you might catch a glimpse of something to help the case. The most interesting thing he and Cooper had seen all day was a lady tripping down some stairs and spilling coffee on herself.

At the same time, he'd kept thinking about Erin, almost obsessively, and he still didn't know how best to approach her.

Either way, Sean was grateful to get out of there.

They marched through the neatly kept parking lot toward the vehicle they'd rented after arriving in town when Cooper's phone rang.

"Hello?" he answered.

Sean couldn't help but listen in to the entire conversation. It was Eric, checking in.

"Progress?" he asked.

"None, whatsoever. We spent all day cooped up in a little room at the health center looking at TV screens."

"So nothing to report at all?" Eric confirmed.

"Well," Cooper began. *Oh God, he's going to tell him about*

Erin now, isn't he?

Sean held his breath and protectively cupped his hand over the pocket containing the paper she'd given him.

"The guy who trained us, Mel, seems like an agreeable sort of chap. Perhaps if we go out for a few pints after shift tomorrow we could question him a bit."

Sean exhaled sharply. He wasn't even sure why the idea of the major finding out about Erin had worried him so.

"Fair enough, right now, report back at the guest house as soon as you can manage. There's someone here to talk to you," Eric said, cutting the call immediately after.

Cooper put the phone away again.

"That was Eric. We have to head back right away. Squad briefing."

Sean nodded. It was probably best if Cooper didn't realize he'd already heard the whole thing. Save for the minor disagreement they'd had about Erin and her true motivations, Sean had got on well with the former Border Agency man. The last thing he needed was to make things awkward between them, when they still had so many more boring days posing as campus security ahead of them.

———◆———

Cooper and Adam and of course Sean himself were already waiting by the time Eric entered the room. "Listen up, everyone!"

Sean looked up to find that Eric had brought company.

The man who stood beside him was unmistakably a fellow shifter.

After hanging out on base with the rest of them, it was obvious now that he'd picked up on their different scents. The stranger standing beside Eric was a bear as well.

"This here is Jamie Abbott. He's the reason we're all here in Inverness."

The squad members all muttered greetings in Jamie's direction.

"Hello," Jamie responded with a nod.

"Off you go," Eric said.

"Okay, well, you already know why I called in the squad. We have two of our own who died under mysterious circumstances. In the past, I might have conducted this investigation myself as part of the Alliance, but seeing as that's your job now, I made a little phone call to Eric here."

Sean frowned. He'd heard of the *New* Alliance before, the shifters who were responsible for outing their entire species to the world. Was that what Jamie was talking about?

"I hear you've already started making inquiries at the University, but only one of the victims was a current student there. I've taken the liberty of making a few calls to get you guys a meeting with the second victim's parents."

Sean nodded. That would be very helpful.

"As always when one of our own dies, the community

is pulling together. It wasn't easy to get a moment with the family alone."

Fair enough.

Eric stepped up beside Jamie and gave him a brotherly pat on the back. "Thank you very much. We'll handle it quickly and respectfully, of course."

Abbott nodded.

"Eric, it would be good if you could take care of it personally. It would mean a lot to the family to have one of our own present."

The two bear shifters shared a look and a handshake.

Sean cleared his throat.

"Yes, McMillan?" Eric asked.

All heads turned in his direction.

"I'd very much like to be present as well."

Eric thought for a moment, then nodded in agreement. "Agreed. Now, we don't want to overwhelm the family, so that's going to have to be it."

Abbott studied Sean for a moment. His expression suggested he wasn't quite sure what to make of him. Sean didn't let it bother him. This wasn't the first time he'd been on the receiving end of a confused look like this. In fact, back in Sevenoaks, when he was still a detective, half of Alpha Squad had stared at him in much the same fashion.

It was the scent thing. Sean was sure of it. One of the guys had let it slip in passing that he smelled human, even though he looked like the rest of them. He wasn't quite sure yet if that was a good or a bad thing.

After what felt like an age, Jamie Abbott finally did look away from him.

"The family will be expecting you in the morning. Now, why don't we go through what you all have found so far," Abbott suggested.

That was inappropriate. Sure, the man had called the squad in, but he seemed awfully comfortable calling the shots.

"It's really too early to tell," Cooper mumbled, earning himself a disapproving look from both Sean as well as Eric.

"We really appreciate you calling us, Jamie," Eric added. "But I'm afraid we're going to have to run this investigation ourselves. We will of course call you first when we find something."

Jamie glared at him, but he didn't protest.

Sean was just glad that he and Eric were on the same page concerning Jamie Abbott's involvement in the case.

"Fine. I understand you have to maintain the integrity of the investigation. It's just that I have a personal stake in this. I am quite close to the Perth family," Jamie explained.

Walter Perth, the second victim, Sean remembered. *Survived by his parents and two younger siblings.*

He waited while Abbott exchanged a few hushed words with Eric. Since they were both shifters, of course they knew to keep their volume down. Even with his equally sensitive hearing, Sean couldn't overhear what was being said from where he stood.

Jamie Abbott excused himself moments later. "I'd better be off."

"Thank you so much for stopping by," Eric said.

The men shook hands again, and soon after, Abbott left the squad room.

"Awkward," Cooper remarked, earning himself yet another disapproving look from Eric.

Sean could hardly suppress a grin. *Every time!* Every single time the man said something or other that he didn't intend for anyone else to hear, only to find that all the shifters on the team could hear him perfectly. And yet he hadn't learned a thing.

"Jamie Abbott is a good man. A capable investigator. His work with the Alliance in Edinburgh was exemplary. It's not his fault that the leadership got things so very wrong at the end," Eric said.

Cooper shrugged. "Okay. Even if I have no idea what this *Alliance* is all about."

Sean was glad it was Cooper who had asked, even though the same question had been burning on his own mind.

"Right. Remember the time before the big reveal? We had our own systems. We couldn't rely on the human government to protect us from the likes of the Sons of Domnall," Eric explained. "The Alliance was formed years ago to protect us from the Sons. Jamie Abbott led their Edinburgh office. That is until the New Alliance—a splinter group formed by some Alliance members in Glasgow—started to rebel against the old Alliance leadership. We recognized that the old ways were no longer viable."

"Okay, cool. Cheers," Cooper said. He looked unimpressed, though that didn't mean much. His expression was equally vacant most of the time.

Eric turned away from the man. He was visibly tense; there was even a slight tremble in his shoulders when he inhaled, as though he was having a hard time keeping calm. Clearly the Alliance and their fight against the Sons was a touchy subject for him.

Eric's phone rang, and he visibly relaxed when he checked the caller ID.

"It's Major Williams."

Sean inhaled sharply. He'd noticed the way those two looked at each other during his time on base. And now Eric sounded downright excited, announcing her call. There was definitely something going on between them.

He scanned the room to gauge the other squad members' reactions, but nobody seemed to have noticed it.

Eric answered, then immediately put the phone on speaker.

"Williams, here. I'd love an update," the major said.

"Well, what did *you guys* find out?" Adam, Eric's brother, spoke up first, if only to raise a question.

Sean and Cooper exchanged a sheepish look.

"Nothing much, to be honest," Sean said. "We underwent training as campus security, and spent much of the afternoon looking at surveillance footage. Sadly, we're assigned to the wrong campus building. You?"

Adam waited for a moment, but when he realized Cooper had nothing to add, he pulled a piece of paper out of his pocket and flattened it against his thigh before handing it to Sean.

"It's not much, but I've been able to make a start on a timeline of Jeremy's—the first victim's—whereabouts during the last few days before his death."

Sean glanced over at Adam, then back at the paper in his hand. This was good work. Pretty much what he would have done, had he been given the chance to interact with the victim's friends.

"Did anyone figure out the truth about you? That you're not really a new student, I mean?" Sean asked.

Adam smiled briefly. "Nah, nobody suspected a thing. Once the topic of Jeremy's untimely death came up, they volunteered much of the information."

Sean frowned. *Talk about lucky.*

"How did you connect with his friend circle so quickly, anyway?" Sean wondered aloud.

"They weren't hard to spot, you know, if you know what you're looking for." Adam grinned.

Of course . Adam had sniffed out the shifters on campus and made an educated guess that they knew the victim. They'd developed an instant connection, simply because

Adam was one of them. *A good investigator makes use of his strengths,* as Sean's training officer had always said back in the day.

Adam's luck was good for the case, of course, though Sean couldn't help being just a little bitter about it. Although he was the only one with proper police training and experience, he wouldn't have been able to get the same results in his place.

Worse still, Sean had achieved nothing all day.

He focused once again on the timeline Adam had handed over.

Everything looked quite normal. Jeremy had mostly gone to class, participated in extracurriculars on campus, hung out with his friends, and visited a local pub in town in the evening. Perhaps they ought to check that place out, in case it had something to do with his death.

"Anything useful there?" Major Williams asked.

Realizing she couldn't read the timeline for herself, Sean proceeded to read it aloud.

Then he looked up, focusing on Adam. "It's promising. I think we should visit this pub, The Castle Tavern. The victim visited it the night before his death. Perhaps someone remembers seeing him."

Of course, his suggestion was just normal police procedure. Track a victim's final movements, visit the places he'd visited in an attempt to find witnesses. The one difference between this case and any normal murder was that they had no idea what really killed him.

The cause of death—heart failure—didn't narrow things down enough. What they really needed was a toxicology report or something—anything—to figure out why the victim ended up dead. Only then would they know how long in advance he might have encountered whatever, or whoever, it was that killed him.

"I suppose there's no chance of us getting another crack at examining the body?" Sean asked.

"We've been through this. Without some concrete evidence, we have nothing to base our request on," the major said.

"But shifters don't just die of heart related problems. Isn't that evidence enough?" Sean questioned.

"You would think so." Major Williams sighed. "But the trouble is there isn't enough knowledge in the mainstream scientific community about shifters and their physiology. Just because these guys here say they've never known any shifter to be affected by these health issues is not going to convince the authorities. It's just anecdotal. We need something more concrete, a smoking gun of sorts."

Sean nodded slowly and passed the paper with Adam's timeline along to Cooper. Major Williams had made an excellent point as usual. If it was him on the other side of this investigation, he wouldn't doubt the word of the medical examiner against a bunch of strangers either. It would take an expert opinion at least, a scientist or a doctor.

"I still think it would be a good idea to make a few inquiries at that pub," Sean said.

Eric nodded in agreement.

"I concur," Major Williams confirmed.

"Where is this place?" Sean turned to face Adam.

"Only a short walk away," Adam said.

"Very well. Good work, Adam. Feel free to take the night. We don't want anyone recognizing you in case any of the victim's friends decide to visit the same pub. Cooper, McMillan, you're up," Eric said.

"Good work, everyone, keep me updated if you find anything else," the major said, ending her call.

CHAPTER FIVE

It was past nine when Erin finally finished typing up the professor's notes. It might as well have been midnight, she felt that shattered.

She packed up her things and gathered up the papers to leave on Blake's desk.

The lab was quiet. Glenn had left at seven, over two hours ago.

But as she turned the corner toward the professor's office, she saw from the crack underneath the door that his light was still on.

She heard muffled voices, though she couldn't tell what they were saying. Perhaps his meeting had run long.

She took a deep breath and knocked.

"Yes?" she heard the professor say.

"Excuse me, I just wanted to leave these notes on your desk before I head home," Erin said as she pushed the door open.

Professor Blake looked frustrated as usual as he beckoned her inside.

Opposite the professor sat a man with salt and pepper hair. As she approached him from behind, he turned around, looking her up and down, before turning his back to her again.

Erin only saw his face for a moment. There was

something familiar about him, but she couldn't remember where she'd seen him before.

"Thank you, Erin. Anything else?"

She shook her head, glancing at the professor's visitor again, but he didn't turn around.

"Good night," she mumbled.

The professor waved her off and focused his attention on his guest, though they didn't start to speak until she pulled the door shut behind herself.

That was weird.

Erin shrugged off her lingering thoughts about who that man might be and started to walk, slowly at first, then faster and faster, until she was practically rushing out into the reception area of the health center. There, she paused.

Behind the reception desk sat just one man, another guard whom Erin had seen many times before. There was no sign of the new recruits. Their shift must have ended already.

This was just the cherry on top of the crappy day Erin had had so far.

Dejected, she started to walk again, much slower this time, toward the exit.

A growl in her stomach reminded her that she hadn't eaten anything since noon. Outside, she picked up her cycle and headed straight for the town center. She wasn't planning on going home just yet, not until she'd had a generous serving of her favorite comfort food: freshly cooked haddock and chips at the pub where Faith waitressed, not far from their shared home.

I earned this, she thought as she pedaled hard to fight the wind. *Hell, I'm still earning it!*

By the time she arrived, ominous black clouds had gathered overhead. The overcast weather made it look later than it actually was; twilight was setting in early tonight.

The pub was a favorite among tourists who'd come to visit the castle just opposite, and due to the incoming weather, the terrace was emptying fast. Inside the establishment, it was crowded and noisy, but Erin didn't let that discourage her. Faith would accommodate her somewhere, even if she had to eat her dinner in the back.

Music was playing, guests were chatting loudly. Everyone seemed to be having a much better night than she did.

Suddenly she recognized a voice through the ruckus. *No way!*

Erin tiptoed to see through the crowd waiting to order at the bar and spotted him. It was the two new guards from work! She wasn't sure whether to be happy about it or not. She *had* made an absolute fool of herself earlier…

"Erin!" Faith called out from across the bar, and pointed at a small, unoccupied table. She wiped her hands on the apron she wore as part of her uniform and smiled warmly at Erin.

"I wasn't expecting you here tonight!"

Erin smiled back, but was unable to muster the same

enthusiasm that seemed to come so naturally to Faith.

Americans… I don't know how they manage being so happy all the time, Erin thought.

"Blake's been running me ragged. You know how it is," Erin mumbled. "I can't be arsed to cook."

"What?" Faith asked, cupping her hand behind her ear.

Erin shook her head and smiled awkwardly again. "Never mind."

Someone was staring at her. She could feel it. And it wasn't just Faith, who was waiting for Erin to order…

Erin looked up in the direction where she'd seen the new guard earlier, and found that he'd spotted her too. A lump developed in her throat, rendering her unable to speak.

Her nerves surged in an instant. At the same time, she couldn't bring herself to look away.

Those eyes… Nearly black in the dim light of the pub.

How intense they looked… hungry.

That thought made Erin frown. She must be imagining things. Perhaps it was the stress getting to her.

"The usual?" Faith asked finally.

Erin nodded, but then changed her mind. "You know what, it's been a long day. Can I get it packed?"

Faith looked slightly disappointed. "Sure thing. Though it won't be as good; you know that, right?"

Erin smiled bleakly. "I'm just really tired tonight."

"Uhuh," Faith said, then glanced over her shoulder at

the guy—Erin's guy. "Well, whatever you want."

If she was really honest with herself, Erin wanted nothing more right now than for the handsome stranger to come over and join her at her table and pretend all the awkwardness earlier at the health center hadn't happened at all. How nice it would be if they could skip all that, start over... He could take her hand, sweep her off her feet with a devilish smile, and wrap his arms around her, and...

Oh God, I'm really losing it now.

Erin shook her head and focused on Faith again. "I'll catch up with you back home, yeah?"

"No problem," Faith responded, and headed straight back to the till, with a spring in her step.

Rather than jump headfirst into more awkwardness, Erin pulled out her phone and started playing around on it aimlessly. He wasn't here for her. If he'd wanted to get in touch, she'd already given him her number.

So whatever this was, a drink with colleagues... She'd be damned if she was going to interrupt it.

Time crawled as she waited for her meal. The two guards, meanwhile, had moved away from their original position at the back of the pub and were talking to Faith now. The way she was smiling at them, and flicking her hair around, suggested she found them attractive too. It was near impossible for Erin to not get jealous that her roomie was getting all the attention and not her.

This is so dumb.

The other guy pulled out his phone and showed Faith

something. Were they sharing jokes now? Faith's serious expression suggested otherwise. She shook her head and said something to the two men which seemed to discourage them.

What the hell had they shown her if not a funny meme or whatever? Her curiosity almost got the better of her, when Faith's supervisor, Clive, arrived at her table carrying a plastic bag.

"Hey Erin. Your food," he said, while handing her a bill.

Erin thanked him and paid straight away. She couldn't wait to get out of here.

Unfortunately, on the way to the door, she had to pass by the two men she'd been wanting to avoid at all costs.

The tall one was looking at her again. She averted her gaze and instead caught a glimpse of the image on the shorter one's phone. Although small, the person it showed was familiar.

Erin froze when she realized who it was.

Jeremy. The young shifter who she'd chatted with at the blood donation camp.

Should she say something? Why were these guys in here showing Faith pictures of Jeremy? The whole situation was weird. Who were they really?

She still felt the tall one's eyes on her, which reminded her why she was getting out of here in the first place. So she kept her observation to herself and rushed out the door.

"Hi," a voice said right behind her.

Erin closed her eyes. She didn't need to turn around to know who it was. Of course, standing here with her back toward him was even more awkward.

She took a deep breath and forced a smile as she turned around.

"Hey."

"I thought I'd say hello," he explained with a shrug.

There was something about him. A certain innocence that drew her in.

"It looked like you were out with your colleague, so I didn't want to interrupt," she said.

"That's okay. I hope you weren't leaving on our account?"

Erin shook her head. "No, no, I was just picking up dinner." She pointed at the bag in her hand.

"I was meaning to call," the stranger said.

Erin pressed her lips together, though that didn't stop her from blurting out whatever was on her mind barely a second later. "Don't worry about it. I wouldn't call me either."

"No, seriously! You need help with that project, so…"

Erin frowned.

"The study you're doing," the man clarified.

"Oh, that. Yes. Well it's okay. That sort of thing isn't everyone's cup of tea. I get it."

"My name's Sean, by the way." He stuck out his hand.

Erin stared at it for a second, before forcing herself into action.

"Erin," she mumbled.

When their hands touched, a jolt of energy passed through her entire body. She forgot to breathe and started to feel faint.

What an idiot she'd been. She didn't want to take blood samples from this guy, or ask him inane questions.

She wanted something entirely different.

But the fact was that he wasn't who he said he was. He was in here asking questions about Jeremy, and Erin wasn't sure she was okay with that.

"Are you alright?" Sean asked.

Erin blinked a few times as she looked up at his face.

"Yeah, great. It's been a long day though. I should head home."

"Right. Yeah. Your dinner must be getting cold as well. So, nice meeting you again," he said.

"Likewise." Erin pulled her hand back, even though she wanted nothing more than to touch him some more. Or more of him.

Oh, shut up, you don't even know the guy!

She forced another smile. "Bye now."

"Bye," he responded.

She turned around and walked to her bike. *Don't look back!*

It took all her self-discipline to follow her own order.

Erin resolutely picked it up, pointed it homeward, and cycled away.

All the while she was certain he was still standing there, looking at her. It was like his eyes were burning holes into her back.

She'd have her dinner and wait for Faith to get home and then she'd ask her all about what Sean and the other guy wanted from her. Something weird was going on, and she was determined to find out more.

By the time she reached home and planted herself in front of the TV, the food had turned soggy. *Bloody typical.*

Faith wouldn't be home for hours. Erin sat back, stuffed a few lukewarm chips in her mouth, and picked up the remote control.

She flipped aimlessly through channels, looking for anything to lift her mood tonight. She paused on a satire show on Channel 4. A panel of comedians was doing funny voice-overs for snippets taken from the news.

Just the ticket to improve her mood.

She put the remote down and took another bite of food, when she paused in her tracks.

Right there in one of the clips she saw a familiar face.

She hit rewind to see the entire segment from the start.

The man who she'd come across in Professor Blake's office today was none other than Victor Domnall, the controversial leader of the anti-shifter group The Sons of Domnall.

What the hell does the professor want with a bigot like him?

Erin pushed the takeaway container aside and picked up her phone to read anything and everything she could find about these people.

The more she found out, the worse she felt. The unexplained optimism she'd felt earlier in the day remained but a distant memory.

Something was very wrong.

CHAPTER SIX

Sean hadn't slept much. He'd been frustrated about the case, or rather his lack of understanding of the case. But that wasn't the true reason for his restlessness.

His second short encounter with Erin had left him more confused than ever.

And every time he'd closed his eyes, attempting to sleep, he'd seen her. As infuriating as his sudden obsession with the woman was, he'd been tempted to just give in and let his mind wander wherever it may.

He'd fantasized about her. And it seemed completely crazy now, in the cold, stark light of day, but he'd imagined a life with her by his side. And he had no idea where all these insane ideas had come from.

Because he'd certainly never felt like this about anyone else.

He wasn't a romantic; he was a realist. And the reality was, they were here to solve two murders, not to find himself a wife.

That last thought stung awkwardly. *A wife.* He didn't even know her! To think of a stranger in such terms was ludicrous.

And she didn't even like him back. Their interactions outside the pub the previous night had told him as much. From the moment she'd spotted him and Cooper, she couldn't wait to get out of there. He wasn't even sure why he'd stopped her as she fled out the door.

"Something bothering you?" Eric asked, as he pulled up in front of a red light.

Sean glanced over at his superior, who sat with one hand nonchalantly draped on top of the steering wheel of their rental car.

He really had to get his head in the game if he didn't want to make people suspicious.

"Yeah, I'm sorry. It's just this case. We still have so many unanswered questions."

Eric nodded. "Well, let's hope the Perth family can help us fill in some of the blanks."

"Hopefully." Sean frowned. "I'm sorry if this is an odd question, but is there something I should be mindful of? Some traditions, or whatever?"

Eric turned around even further with a puzzled expression on his face. "They're grieving the loss of their son, I'm not sure what else you could be referring to."

Sean sighed. *Stupid question, stupid answer.*

"Look, I'm going to be completely straight with you," he said.

"Okay..."

Now or never. If he couldn't confide in Eric, of all people, then what hope was there for him on this squad?

"I'm not one of you guys," Sean began. "Not really."

Eric frowned. One of the cars behind them honked,

reminding them that the lights had turned.

Sean waited as Eric pulled away and they had hit a more open stretch of road.

"I basically grew up human. Sure, I can shift, technically, but that wasn't something we talked about at home. My dad…" Sean looked out the window, just so he wouldn't have to see Eric's reaction to what he was telling him. They'd just crossed the edge of town, and the dramatic mountain landscape typical of this part of the Highlands opened up ahead of them. The beauty of the land here was equally distracting, so Sean focused on the dashboard instead.

"When he met my mother, he chose to life a human life. I'm not sure she even knew. When I turned thirteen and I noticed a few things about myself that didn't seem quite normal, he explained everything to me. That was it. One conversation. There wasn't any room for questions. I don't know about a whole lot of things you guys take for granted."

Eric exhaled sharply. "Okay, McMillan. That does explain a lot."

Sean waited for more of a reaction, but instead it was the GPS that interrupted the silence.

"You will reach your destination in 400 yards."

"Let's focus on interviewing the family," Sean suggested.

Eric nodded. "Indeed. But I appreciate you telling me all this. I'll bear it in mind." He turned into a small driveway leading to the only house on this stretch of road. This had to be it.

They shared a quick look of understanding, then got out of the car.

Although it had been awkward for Sean to admit all that, he felt relieved. He really wasn't one of them, and it was best at least Eric knew it.

Eric approached the front door of the stone cottage and was just about to knock, when it swung open.

An elderly couple awaited them inside.

"You must be the lads Jamie told us about," the woman said in a low, frail voice.

The man didn't say anything, just stepped aside, letting Eric and Sean in.

"Eric King, Alpha Squad. I'm so sorry about your son," Eric said. "This is my associate, Sean McMillan."

"My condolences," Sean said, shaking first the woman's, then the man's hand. "We'll do everything we can to get to the bottom of this."

He knew better than to make promises he couldn't keep.

They followed the couple inside, through the hall and into the living room.

"Why don't you take a seat?" The victim's mother gestured at one of the sofas. On the coffee table in front of it, cups, saucers, and even a kettle were already waiting.

"Thank you," Eric said.

Sean nodded and took a seat. He made it a point whenever he went to someone's house—whether it was a victim, a witness, or a suspect—to really observe his surroundings.

From the family photos on the mantle, to the stack of mail on the dining table in the other section of the room, the decor was as one would expect for a cottage owned by a couple in their seventies. From the sofas, to the drapes, earthy colors and floral prints prevailed.

It was cozy. Had he not already known, he would have never been able to tell whether shifters or humans lived in this house.

"What is it you want to know," the man finally spoke up. His voice was raw with grief.

This was the worst part of the job, but Sean found comfort in the thought that he could do his part in uncovering the truth and perhaps help these people find closure.

"Why don't you tell us exactly what happened," Eric started.

The man's face grew even tenser. "He died, that's what happened."

Sean leaned forward in his seat. "We know this will be difficult to talk about, and we apologize for that, but what happened during the hours leading up to Walter's death? How was his state of mind? Did he complain of any discomfort at all? This all will help us work out what exactly might have happened to him."

The man sighed and rested his head in his hands. "He was fine. Everything was fine. He was here for dinner the night before. That was the last time we saw him. Next thing we know, the police turns up to tell us he's gone."

Sean pulled out a small notepad and started scribbling down the basics of what Mr. Perth had said.

"What about earlier in the week. Had he gone anywhere unusual, or done anything out of the ordinary. Maybe he'd met with someone new? Anything you can remember would be helpful."

"How would we know? He was a grown man, for God's sake! We didn't keep track of everything he was up to."

Sean nodded patiently, then diverted his attention to Mrs. Perth, who had just been sitting quietly in the armchair across from her husband. Her hands were trembling as she held on to her cup of tea.

"Did he mention anything to you perhaps? Even an offhand comment could help," he asked.

She blinked a few times. Sticky eyelashes framed already puffy eyelids.

"Look, we want to get to the bottom of this. And Jamie assured us you're here to help. But this isn't helping. You've upset my wife all over again. I think it's best if you leave." Mr. Perth got up from his seat and gestured at the door.

Eric got up immediately and headed for the door. Sean

leaned forward some more, and leaned his elbows on his knees as he addressed the victim's mother again.

"We really are very sorry for what happened to your son. Anything at all you can remember?"

She shook her head. "Oh, I don't know! If only I knew something that could help."

"That's enough. Come on," Eric urged.

It was time to admit defeat.

"Very well. If you think of anything, feel free to call." He pulled a business card out of his pocket and handed it to her.

On his way out, he continued to take in as much as he could. He noticed the water stains on the wallpaper underneath the windowsill. The potted plants that had been much loved until recently, but not anymore; the soil was dry and the leaves were starting to wilt.

A piece of yellow paper, folded up, resting on the side table underneath a bunch of keys. That color!

Sean reached into his back pocket and pulled out the paper Erin had written her phone number on when they'd first met. It looked just like the one on the side table. *Coincidence?*

He turned around and held it up to Mrs. Perth. "Have you seen this before?"

She frowned and took the leaflet from him, reading the heading. "Yes… Yes indeed! Walt told me about this. He'd gone and donated blood himself!"

"What's this, then?" Mr. Perth approached and studied

the leaflet himself. "Do you think something happened to him there?"

Eric frowned and observed the exchange. Sean would explain it to him in the car.

"It's too early to tell, but it gives us a starting point," Sean said, folding the paper up and putting it back in his pocket. "Thank you so much for your help."

"Whatever you say," Mr. Perth said.

Sean remained quiet in the car while Eric started the engine.

"What was that all about?" Eric asked as he pulled out of the driveway.

"Maybe nothing," Sean said. His mind was working overtime.

Last night at the pub, Erin had seen the photo Cooper had shown to the waitress. He'd watched her as she stared at it just a bit too long for comfort.

She'd recognized the first victim.

And now there was a potential connection between her and the second victim as well?

It was a small town, but Sean didn't believe in coincidences. She'd acted strangely too, the way she'd almost run away from him when she'd been the one to initiate contact during their first meeting. Something had spooked her or changed her mind. What was it?

Was she onto them?

And then there was all that stuff Cooper had said about

her. How she seemed a bit too keen to talk to them at first. Like she wasn't being upfront about what she wanted.

Sean didn't want to think ill of her. But something strange was going on in this town, and he had but one goal: to uncover the truth.

"Let's talk to Adam," Sean suggested.

Eric shrugged. "Sure, but I'm not clear on where you're going with this."

"Maybe he can find out if the first victim had been anywhere near that blood donation drive as well. Maybe that's the connection," Sean said.

"Fine, go ahead." Eric nodded in agreement.

Sean retrieved his phone from his pocket and dialed Adam's number, then put the phone on speaker.

"Hello?" Adam answered on the other end.

"Hello mate. Can you talk? Are you alone?" Sean asked, mindful that if he was around the first victim's friends—fellow shifters—their phone conversation would not be private.

"Yeah, but make it quick," Adam said.

"Okay, I need you to find out if Jeremy attended a blood donation drive on campus a few days before he died," Sean said.

"You have a lead?" Adam asked.

"It's too early to tell," Eric butted in.

"Cool. I'll let you know." Adam cut the call.

Sean put the phone away again, and his fingers brushed past the paper.

Perhaps he should call Erin, and subtly question her about her involvement.

CHAPTER SEVEN

As hard as Erin had tried to stay awake, she was fast asleep by the time Faith got home.

And come morning, of course Faith wasn't up yet by the time Erin had to leave for work, leaving them no time to catch up.

It hadn't been a restful sleep, though. Erin had tossed and turned, tormented by nightmares, none of which she could remember after waking up.

Obviously, all of the events of the previous day were catching up with her.

She hated not knowing what those new guys from work had said to Faith exactly. And what about Professor Blake meeting with none other than Victor Domnall?

The man was dangerous. His entire agenda seemed to be to stir up hate and violence against one specific minority living among them: shifters.

What could such a person possibly want with Professor Blake?

Erin's boss was unpleasant at the best of times, but she'd never considered that he might hold similar, controversial beliefs. He was a scientist after all, as she was.

But the ideologies Domnall promoted—as far as she was concerned—were just fear-mongering nonsense. They were not based in logic or fact.

He was nothing more than a common racist.

And this morning, over a steaming hot cup of coffee, Erin found herself wondering who the professor really was. Had she unknowingly been working for some crazy fanatic? What else didn't she know?

She needed answers and wasn't sure who she could turn to.

As Erin left the house, the weather was predictably ominous. The clouds that had collected in the valley overnight had only grown denser. There was a certain heaviness in the air, meaning it was only a matter of time before it would rain.

Erin wore waterproofs just in case.

Yesterday had started on such a bright note for her, but today she felt the opposite.

She arrived at the health center windblown and five minutes late. If Blake was there, her delayed arrival would earn her a lecture. She could only hope she could keep calm and not blurt out something she would regret.

Thankfully, by the time she made it into the lab, only Glenn was there.

"Morning," she said.

"Morning." He only acknowledged her for a moment.

Rather than walk past his desk and mind her own business, she paused in the doorway. There was nobody else here. And Glenn had been with Professor Blake a lot longer than she had. If anyone could provide answers, it was him.

"Say…" Erin started. "What do you think it is we're actually working on here?"

Glenn frowned and pushed his keyboard aside.

She'd crossed a line and she knew it. Still, they were colleagues, right? They were in the same boat together.

"What do you mean?" he asked.

"Well, he's such a famous researcher, it's got to be something exciting, right?"

Glenn shrugged. "Look, I just come in every morning and mind my own business."

"Right…" Erin said. "I'm just trying to make conversation. It gets pretty lonely in here, you know? It's nice to have a chat every so often."

Glenn slowly shook his head. Clearly, he could not relate to Erin's observation.

"So, what are *you* working on then?" she said. "Anything exciting?"

"I'm sequencing these samples," Glenn said, pointing at the large machine sitting towards the right of his computer. Erin could hear it hum all the way from the door.

"Samples of what?"

"How would I know? I just put it in the sequencer and let it do its thing. Professor Blake will look at the results when it's done."

Erin folded her arms. So Glenn had no clue what was

going on either, or he had no intention of telling her anything.

"Oh well. Thanks," she said.

Glenn shrugged and focused on his computer once more.

That was as clear a signal as Erin needed. This conversation was over.

She walked towards her workstation and put her bag down beside her chair. She'd better get to work if she wanted to avoid future unpleasantness from the professor regarding her lack of productivity.

She pulled out a notepad to scribble down ideas to publicize the second blood drive Blake wanted to organize. It had been her idea to also get people signed up as organ donors. She pulled up the relevant government website and downloaded posters and other material.

This was a cause Erin genuinely believed in. Despite the unsettling doubts she woke up with this morning, time passed more quickly now that she was working on this project.

Whoever Blake was, it was these little side projects that allowed her to make a difference. That was why she'd studied to become a scientist. So she could help people somehow. To give her life meaning, something she'd been struggling to find since the death of both her parents two years ago.

It was almost noon by the time she looked up from the

pile of work on her desk. She'd more than earned a cup of tea.

As Erin waited for the kettle to boil, her mind started to wander again. The last blood drive had been such a big success, and her chance meeting with Jeremy had sparked a whole new area of interest for her. Was shifter blood any different from normal human blood?

Doctors had pre-screened everyone to make sure they were suitable donors, so presumably Jeremy's blood was just fine.

If only she'd been able to keep a sample… It was that same wishful thinking which had inspired her to try to talk that guy, Sean, into helping her out. Only she had no idea who he really was or what he was doing here.

Back to Jeremy. Why had Sean's buddy shown Faith Jeremy's picture last night at the pub?

Erin hadn't seen Jeremy since the blood drive last week. Of course, students didn't frequent this place much, unless they were part of a research project or interning here, so that in itself wasn't unusual.

Was he in trouble? Were those men looking for him because he'd done something wrong?

Or had something happened to him?

It was this second thought which filled Erin with dread. He'd seemed like such a nice guy.

She flinched when her phone rang. Perhaps it was Faith, calling for a chat.

The number on screen wasn't familiar though.

Probably a telemarketer.

"Hello?" she said sternly.

There was a moment of silence on the other end, almost causing her to hang up, but then a familiar voice spoke.

"Hello, Erin."

Holy hell, it was Sean.

"Uh, hi!" she said, immediately regretting how excited her greeting had sounded.

"Told you I'd call."

He *had* said that. But Erin couldn't shake the feeling that he had an ulterior motive.

"Are you calling to tell me you're participating in my research project?" she asked. Embarrassing or not, it was best to keep this conversation as professional as possible.

There was another pause. *That'll be a no, then.*

"Why don't we discuss it in person? I'm assuming you're off for lunch soon?" he asked.

Erin swallowed, hard. This was unexpected.

And awkward.

"Yeah," she started. "I don't know…"

"Come on, I hear the cafeteria here sells the most amazing roast beef sandwiches."

Erin scoffed. The cafeteria was so notoriously bad, only visitors ate there.

"Did Mel tell you that? Don't believe a word he says. I think we can do better," Erin said.

Sean laughed and Erin couldn't suppress a smile either.

Was she honestly flirting with the guy now? She didn't even know what he wanted from her. As much as her mind questioned his motives, her gut tried to tell her to trust him.

"Well then, meet me out in the lobby. When do you get off for lunch?" he asked.

Erin checked her watch. She normally ate at her desk whenever she got hungry, so she didn't have a fixed time. Still, she shouldn't sound too eager.

"Half an hour?" she asked.

"Brilliant. See you then." Sean cut the call.

Erin stared at her phone for a moment. That was weird. Despite her concerns about his true purpose here, she was excited about seeing him again.

She returned to her desk to finish her cup of tea. Now that this was actually happening, she'd better be prepared. Perhaps she should just flat-out ask him what he wanted with Jeremy. They'd seemed to have a bit of a rapport outside the pub last night. Maybe he would let something slip.

Or was it best to be subtle about it? Erin couldn't decide.

When she left the lab and headed down the hall towards reception, she still wasn't sure how to handle him. All she knew was that the prospect of lunch together was giving her butterflies in her stomach.

He was already waiting. God, was he handsome, even

in that silly rent-a-cop uniform.

"Hi, Erin," he greeted her with a smile.

She smiled and nodded. Should she ask him about Jeremy now? Or not at all?

"So, where are we going?" he asked.

Erin blinked a few times. She hadn't actually thought about *that*.

"There's a place just down the road. It's walking distance…" she suggested.

He nodded and opened the door for her.

"Thanks," Erin mumbled.

She stole a glance at him as he walked beside her. She should definitely ask him now. *Stop being such a coward!*

He stuck his hand in his pocket, and pulled something out. A yellow piece of paper.

"Can you tell me about this?" he asked.

Erin stopped and inspected the leaflet. It was from last week's blood donation drive.

"Where did you get this?" she asked.

He smiled and turned it over. Her phone number was written on the back.

Of course!

"Right," she said. "Why do you want to know about this?"

She took the leaflet from him, and in the process her finger brushed past his hand. Her heart beat so fast she thought it might explode.

Then, out of nowhere, something inside her changed.

She felt heavy-hearted, like something bad was going to happen. Or perhaps it already had.

"What's going on?" she whispered, as she gave the leaflet back to him.

Sean looked down at her. His eyes were fixed on hers. Like they were trying to tell her something, but she wasn't sure what it was.

"I'm only posing as a security guard," he said. His voice was low, serious.

Erin rubbed her arms, trying to make the goosebumps go down.

"I know that." She'd said it without even thinking if it was wise of her to admit.

"Have you heard of Alpha Squad?" he asked.

What the hell is Alpha Squad?

Before she had the chance to voice her question aloud, he started to speak again. "Alpha Squad is a government task force set up by the Ministry of Shifter Affairs. We investigate shifter related matters."

Erin blinked a few times. First Victor Domnall shows up in Professor Blake's office, now this. Something was definitely going on, and she had landed right in the middle of it.

"What happened to Jeremy?" she blurted out.

"Jeremy… You knew him?" Sean rested his hand on her shoulder. "You look pale, are you alright?"

"Why are you talking about him in past tense?" Erin

whispered.

"Oh, you didn't know!" Sean said. "Come here, let's sit down." He pointed at a nearby wooden bench.

Erin did as she was told, while her mind was racing out of control. Something had happened to Jeremy. That was what Sean was here to investigate.

"He passed away last week. Although he appeared to have died of natural causes, we suspect foul play," Sean said.

"No! He was so young! What happened?" Erin asked, her fingers tightening around the edge of the seat.

"We're not quite sure. He was healthy one moment, and his heart failed suddenly." Sean pointed at the leaflet in his hand again. "Could you tell me about this? It might help."

"That's where I met Jeremy. He came in to donate blood, and I attended to him."

Sean reached into his pocket again and took out his phone. "Did you see this man also?" he asked, showing her a picture of a blond-haired guy who looked to be in his mid-twenties.

Erin shook her head slowly. "I don't know. A lot of people came in that day. I know for sure that he didn't come to my station. Why, who is he?"

Sean sighed deeply. "Another victim. The same thing happened to him; he died of sudden heart failure. We believe they both donated blood that day. It's the only real connection between the two of them. Well, that, and they're both shifters."

Erin pressed her lips together tightly. *This cannot be happening.*

"Don't worry, there's no reason to believe you're in danger," Sean said.

Erin shook her head. "That's not what I'm worried about at all."

"Oh?"

"I suspect my boss is involved in this. I don't know how he did it. But…" Erin whispered. "I saw something last night that's been bothering me and I didn't know who to tell."

"Tell me."

"I saw him meet with Victor Domnall, that anti-shifter guy, in his office yesterday. That can't be a coincidence, can it?"

Erin rested her head in her hands. The tears came almost immediately, but they brought no relief. She'd always been a practical sort of person. She believed in cause and effect, not coincidences.

Her seeing Victor Domnall with Professor Blake, and this case Sean was investigating had to be related. And if the blood drive had something to do with it, so did she.

CHAPTER EIGHT

When Sean called Erin to ask her out to lunch, he'd just planned to subtly question her about that blood drive. The conversation had taken a very unexpected turn indeed.

How helpless he felt. The news about Jeremy, the first victim, had affected her deeply.

And he could do nothing to help.

"Come on now, it's going to be okay," he mumbled.

Erin looked up through smudged eyelashes. "How? My boss killed two people that we know of! I'm guilty by association, or worse!"

If you put it that way…

Sean remembered what Cooper had said, about her approaching them in the lobby the previous day. Like she was up to something.

But now that he saw her reaction, it didn't seem possible for her to be involved. She had no idea what was going on. It was as if he could *feel* her.

Her sorrow; her guilt.

Sean took a deep breath to try to maintain his composure.

"What do you mean, or worse?" he asked.

Erin folded her hands in her lap and stared at the ground.

"If these were murders, then Jeremy and the other man

must have come into contact with something or other, like a poison. Or a pathogen. Something that their bodies couldn't tolerate."

"Right, that's what we were thinking," Sean said.

"If the only connection between them was the blood donation camp, then it follows that they got infected there."

"True."

"I was there. I spoke to Jeremy. I put the needle in his arm. What if…" Her sentence was cut short by a loud sob. "What if *I* did it? What if *I'm* responsible?"

Sean didn't know what to say. He closed his eyes and let her pain wash over him.

This wasn't his first case, not even his most tragic one. He'd never had trouble keeping his emotions in check during an investigation. But this time, it seemed impossible. He couldn't detach himself from her.

It felt terrible, like his heart had been ripped out from his chest. And it wasn't empathy that he felt.

This was something else; they'd formed a connection he couldn't explain.

He reached for her hand, half expecting that she'd pull it away. She didn't.

She just sat there, crying in complete silence, mourning the deaths of two people she didn't even know, not really.

By her own account, she'd met Jeremy once and Walter not at all.

"I have to make this right," she whispered.

"What?" Sean asked.

"I have to fix this. I don't know how, but I have to do something," she said.

"I understand why you feel that way, but we don't even know what killed them. Maybe we're on the wrong track and your boss had nothing to do with it at all." He wasn't even sure why he was telling her that. He sure as hell didn't believe it.

Moments earlier, Erin had provided the biggest break in the case so far. It was obvious they were on the right track.

"Even if he did, you didn't know. None of this is your fault, Erin!"

Erin shook her head. "I have to… I have to help you find out what happened."

Sean pressed his lips together. He had to shake it off. Get rid of all these messy feelings. She'd identified herself as a potential suspect, and here he was, holding her hand, consoling her like it was the most normal thing in the world.

And she wanted to insert herself into the case as well. *No way.* This was extremely unprofessional. He should keep his distance from her.

But instead of pulling away, he wrapped his arm around her and pulled her into his arms.

Why does anyone want to kill shifters? What have they ever done?

Sean flinched backwards and released her.

What the hell was that? Who said that?

You can hear me?

Erin looked up at him, her eyes wide with shock.

He didn't know what to say either.

She was in his head. He was in hers.

Without knowing why or how, they were reading each other's thoughts.

Sean got up and ran his hand through his hair, before starting to pace back and forth.

"You heard that too, right?" he asked.

"Yeah… I thought I was imagining it," Erin mumbled.

He shook his head. This was impossible. He expected that at any moment he might wake up and realize this had all just been a bizarre dream. Of course, nothing of the sort happened.

It started to rain, and the cool droplets helped ground him. This was real. As real as the earth beneath his feet and the clouds emptying themselves above them.

"Is this a weird shifter thing?" Erin asked, while wiping her face with the back of her hand.

Sean took another step back. *How do you know I'm a shifter?*

Erin cocked her head to the side. *You just said you're with Alpha Squad, a government task force for shifters!*

He stared at her for a moment. It had happened again. He'd thought something, and she'd answered, right there in his head. Unnerving couldn't quite describe how he felt.

The privacy of his mind was no longer just his anymore.

So is Cooper, and he isn't a shifter! Sean thought.

Erin glanced away again and shrugged. *I thought… You look like one… Forget it.*

His whole life he'd passed for human, both in human as well as shifter company. And now Erin came along and told him he *looked* like a shifter. Just like that.

He took a deep breath and closed his eyes for a moment.

"Why did you approach Cooper and me yesterday?" Sean asked.

Erin refused to look him in the eye.

Tell me, please! Sean thought.

Because I felt drawn to you. That doesn't even make sense, does it?

Strangely enough, it made perfect sense to him. He'd felt the same from the moment he first saw her.

He ought to tell her to back off. To leave the investigation to him and the squad.

I can get you in. Perhaps we'll find something in the lab, together? Her voice was back in his thoughts again.

Sean licked his lips and stared at her for a moment.

Windblown hair and puffy eyes couldn't diminish her beauty. The more fragile she looked, the stronger the urge was to protect her. If he could be the reason for her to smile again, wouldn't that be worth every sacrifice?

The blue depths of her eyes spoke the truth.

The voice he heard in his mind could tell no lies.

Her guilt continued to tug at him. To refuse her the chance to help… It would be cruel.

"I would welcome the chance to investigate the lab, and right now we have nothing to justify a warrant," Sean mumbled.

Erin got up and dusted herself off. "Then it's decided. We go in together."

He didn't like the idea, not really. But what choice was there?

Sean checked his watch. It was barely quarter to one.

"What time do you guys get off work normally?" he asked.

"Five-thirty, officially, but office hours hold no real meaning here. Glenn, my colleague, will probably leave by seven. As for the professor, who knows? I haven't seen him all day, though."

Sean nodded. "Cooper and I are on shift until seven, but I don't think anyone will question me if I stay late. Not as long as I'm wearing this uniform."

"So I'll stay behind after Glenn leaves and signal you."

"I'll make sure to do my final round of the building past Professor Blake's office, to make sure he's not around," Sean said.

They had the beginnings of a plan. But what they were looking for exactly, Sean had no idea. Not to mention that it was highly unprofessional and even illegal.

"So you were saying, about what could have done it. A

toxin or a pathogen?" he asked.

Erin nodded. *If the blood drive was the point of contact, it has to be something that doesn't affect humans, or there would have been a lot more victims.*

"So we're looking for something that specifically attacks shifters."

"Any thoughts? Is there anything you guys are specifically sensitive to?" Erin asked.

Sean pressed his lips together and slowly shook his head. "I honestly have no idea."

"Well, do you have a doctor or someone on your squad who might know?" Erin continued.

The despair that had been so evident in her eyes before had dissipated now that she was steering her thoughts toward a solution. She needed this puzzle, this chance to uncover the truth. They weren't so different after all.

As unethical as it was to involve her, he'd do anything not to see her in so much anguish again.

His objectivity had well and truly gone out the window on this one.

"We don't have anyone like that," Sean answered.

Erin frowned. "You should."

"What I mean is, I'm not sure someone like that exists. There is no literature, no research to consult. They—I mean, we—don't get sick. We don't need doctors."

Erin stared up at him, her eyes full of wonder. "Really? That's amazing. I mean, wow."

"I guess so," he mumbled.

"Seriously. To not have to worry about getting sick, that's a big deal."

All his life he'd dealt with suspicion; as a child, his classmates had kept their distance because he was so much taller and stronger than any of them. As a detective, he'd dealt mostly with people who wanted nothing better than to avoid his company.

And those were just the humans.

The shifters he'd come into contact with since Alpha Squad hadn't fully accepted him either.

Erin was different though. The way she'd looked at him had made him uneasy at first. But now he recognized it as admiration.

Perhaps even love.

No, that would be ridiculous.

What is? her voice asked.

Sean closed his eyes and tried to fight the emotions that threatened to overwhelm.

It was no use.

Her scent tempted him.

Her mere presence had made him agree to things he would have never considered otherwise.

Why can I feel you so keenly now? When earlier I couldn't, he thought.

I don't know, but I'm glad for this.

Sean looked down at her again. Her face was still wet.

A soft drizzle started, depositing gleaming little

droplets in her bright red hair.

She was a vision. A Scottish beauty that could inspire legends.

With hands that had grown a mind of their own, he reached for her. Cupping her face, leaning down to meet her lips with his.

She didn't resist, but rather seemed to melt against him.

How could a touch feel so powerful? His fingertips on her moist cheeks.

His kiss merging into hers.

Their minds had become one already. Those deepest, darkest parts of himself which he'd fought an entire lifetime to keep hidden wanted more.

This is inappropriate. You're a suspect.

I'm your partner.

Sean inhaled sharply, letting her perfume fill his lungs. Sweet, like a summer meadow.

Yes. Yes, you are.

Every fiber in his body agreed. They were one in thought. It was only a matter of time before they'd become one in flesh.

With all the self-control he could manage, he pulled away from her. This wasn't the place, nor the time.

It wasn't the kind of man he was either.

She stood frozen in place for a moment, her eyes still closed, her beautiful face a mask of calm.

"Let's get out of here before anyone takes notice," Sean

suggested. "I still owe you lunch."

Erin shook her head. "After everything, I'm not hungry anymore."

Sean nodded. She needed to process what had just happened. That was understandable.

I'm sorry.

We'll get to the bottom of this, I promise, he tried to reassure her.

They said their goodbyes, awkwardly.

See you later.

I can't wait.

As Sean watched her walk away, he tried to regain control. He'd given her too much. He'd accepted her help and they would investigate the lab together.

But there'd be no more of this. Sean licked his lips, briefly. He could still taste her.

This was unacceptable. No matter how beautiful she was, or how strongly he felt about her. He couldn't let it happen again, not until the case was over.

CHAPTER NINE

Erin couldn't believe how her unexpected lunch date had turned out.

She sat down at her desk, still trembling after that first kiss with Sean. But when she closed her eyes, and ran the tip of her index finger over her lips, it wasn't all pleasurable.

They'd found each other. They'd confessed their attraction and sealed it with a kiss.

At the same time, she'd received the worst news anyone could ever hear. Her work with Professor Blake was tainted. All the hours she'd poured into making that blood drive a success... It was that event and those like it which had been the silver lining to her otherwise bleak existence inside this lab. And now, she didn't even have that to hold onto anymore.

He'd used her, and hurt, even killed people in the process.

Her one reason for getting into this line of work was helping people. He'd taken that ideal and perverted it. Because of one crazy old man, she potentially had blood on her hands too.

Erin glanced at the folder she'd prepared earlier. All those ideas to make the next blood and organ donation event a success.

Without giving it further thought, she brushed the entire lot off her desk and into the dustbin that stood beside it.

Her work here had come to an end. She'd fake it, just long enough to make it through the evening so she could help Sean, but that was it.

She wouldn't be complicit in the evil Blake was involved in.

She wouldn't stand by and allow him to hurt any more people.

Throughout the afternoon, Erin found it hard to remain calm. She'd tried to distract herself by playing solitaire on her computer, but it hadn't helped much.

If the professor turned up, what would she say to him? Would she be able to keep her emotions in check? Or would she blow the entire thing right then and there?

Thankfully, she never had to find out.

At seven, sharp, Erin heard a squeak in the other room. That was Glenn, getting up from his seat.

He'd do the same thing he always did in the evening: pack up his belongings into the messenger bag he carried, switch off his computer and the lights in his cubicle, then double and triple-check all the equipment to make sure it was off.

In all, the ritual would take about five minutes.

Then he'd leave, probably without saying goodbye. Erin kept her eyes fixed on the clock on her phone, counting down the seconds and minutes, while listening to

Glenn move around in the other room.

The sounds stopped. He'd be gone any moment now.

"You're still here?" Glenn's voice made her flinch.

She turned around and forced a smile, hoping he hadn't noticed just how much his question had startled her. "Yeah, I'm just finishing up the plans for that organ donation event. The professor wanted it today."

Glenn nodded.

Oh please, let him leave right now. The lab was silent, except for the subtle hum of Erin's PC. Her heart was hammering away in her ears loud enough she could swear Glenn would have heard it too.

Glenn paused for a moment, as though he had something else to say, but then shrugged and walked off.

Erin breathed a sigh of relief when the main door to the lab closed behind him. What a day for Glenn to develop a sense of curiosity about her comings and goings. No doubt she'd brought this on herself with her intrusive questions in the morning.

She waited for another ten minutes or so, before finally sending Sean a message.

The coast is clear. You can come by now.

Erin put the phone down and waited, her heart racing even faster now.

She'd followed the rules all her life—that was just the kind of person she was. Tonight, though, she was facilitating a break-in.

A necessary evil.

But what if they got caught? Maybe Sean's affiliation with Alpha Squad gave them some leeway.

Erin held her breath, then exhaled deeply when Sean pushed open the same door Glenn had just left from earlier.

"Blake?" she asked.

Sean shook his head. "His office is empty, it looks like he hasn't been there all day."

Erin sighed and pushed her chair back. "Let's do this, then." *The sooner we get out of here, the better.*

Sean nodded.

They were on the same page. *Soul mates.*

Erin suppressed a smile. This was so not the right time to be thinking like that. Especially when the one she was thinking about could hear her every thought!

Sean didn't react to that last thought of hers. In fact, he was acting rather stiff and distant. Like their kiss earlier had never even happened. *He's just focusing on the job at hand,* Erin tried to reassure herself, but it stung nonetheless.

"So, what have you been working on here?" Sean asked.

Erin sighed and shook her head. "That's just it. I have no idea what the professor has been doing. I transcribe his notes, but they're all meaningless since I don't know what they're about."

She pulled open one of the drawers underneath her

desk and took out a stack of handwritten papers the professor had left with her. They were tables and tables of figures, formulas, and calculations which were meaningless without context.

"See, here. He's been doing tests and experiments. But I don't know what he's been looking for."

Sean glanced at the notes, then scanned the rest of the lab. "What's in there?" He nodded at Glenn's cubicle.

"That's where we keep the sequencer. For DNA testing." Erin put the notes back and closed the drawer again. "That's Glenn's domain."

"And in there?" Sean pointed at the freezer in the corner.

"Blood samples."

"Whose blood?" Sean asked.

Erin shrugged. She'd gotten him into the lab, but it was painfully obvious that she had very little knowledge of what was going on here. "I don't know," she whispered.

"Right, well, he may not have told you what he was up to, but I'm sure everything we need is right here or in his office," Sean said.

If he was disappointed in her, his tone didn't show it. Neither did it carry any other, more positive emotion.

"Do you know how that machine works? The sequencer?"

"Of course, but it'll take hours to test a sample."

Sean looked around again, completely avoiding eye

contact with her. "What else can we do in here?"

He's just focusing on the case, Erin told herself.

Erin got up and entered Glenn's cubicle. Perhaps he'd left something lying around that could prove helpful. She switched on his PC and waited for it to boot up.

She breathed a sigh of relief when his desktop came into view. No password protection, nothing. Perhaps Glenn wasn't involved after all. He hadn't even bothered to secure his data.

"Let's see if I can pull up past results from the sequencer," Erin said.

Sean joined her and watched over her shoulder as she sat down on Glenn's chair and started searching through the folders on his hard drive.

The data she was after was right there, categorized by date and an ID number that meant nothing to her.

Erin opened a few of the reports and started analyzing the results.

Sean waited in silence.

She'd looked at so many charts like this during her studies, but unless he had something to compare these to, she wouldn't know what she was looking at exactly. All she could definitively tell at first glance was that these results belonged to complex organisms: mammals, possibly even people.

She closed the reports again and started studying the folders they were organized in. The same few ID numbers were repeated over and over.

If she assumed that an ID belonged to a specific subject, this meant he was sequencing the same DNA multiple times. Why would he do that? DNA didn't just change; the results would be the same every time.

She pulled a blank sheet of paper out of the printer tray and started to make a chart. In it she recorded the dates each ID number had been tested. The results were confusing.

"Assuming these numbers identify patients, or test subjects, he's doing weekly tests on a whole lot of them," Erin said, looking up. "Some of these go back months! But then, here's one for example, which was mentioned for the first time last week."

"Okay, so he's running an experiment of sorts. To alter DNA?" Sean asked.

Erin nodded. It did seem so. But where was he getting these samples from? And why were some being tested week after week for months, while others appeared only recently?

"I wonder if these numbers correspond to the samples I've prepped recently," Erin wondered aloud.

She got up and rummaged through the freezer back in her section of the lab and compared the labels to her handwritten chart.

The results were telling.

"I don't have samples from any of the older subjects. Only the four he's added last week."

What does it mean?

Sean folded his arms. "That blood donation drive was last week," he observed. "Could he have kept some of the blood for his own study?"

She couldn't believe she hadn't made the connection herself. What better place to get new blood samples without anyone questioning it!

Erin thought back to that day. For every donation she'd taken, she'd labeled the pouch herself and kept it in the appropriate containers for transport to the nearest hospital. But she hadn't actually overseen the transports herself; the professor had been in charge of that.

He could have very easily tampered with the containers and taken some of the pouches for himself.

But they'd taken blood from hundreds of people that day, and yet only a handful of new ID numbers had appeared in the reports on Glenn's computer. How had he made his selection?

He was targeting shifters, so perhaps he'd only taken samples from those he suspected weren't fully human?

Erin sat down on a stool near the freezer and stared at the slides still in her hand, and back at the chart. *Did one of these numbers identify Jeremy's blood? What about the other guy, Walter?*

"I don't think we'll learn anything more here," Sean spoke softly, and rested his hand on her shoulder. "Not without knowing more specifics about what he's studying."

For a moment, Sean's touch caught her off guard. She

wanted him, to feel connected to him like she had outside at lunchtime.

But she wanted to redeem herself more.

Erin's jaw tightened. No, she wasn't ready to admit defeat yet. "We can look at these properly, under a microscope I mean," she said, pointing at the slides. "We can compare the DNA results of the new ID numbers to the older ones. I'm not leaving here until I get a copy of everything I can get my hands on."

Sean shrugged and took a seat. "If you think it'll help." He sounded distant again. This hot and cold vibe she was getting from him was only adding to her frustrations.

Still, she was determined to follow through on her plan. If she studied the evidence, she was bound to uncover the truth. And it would finally give her the chance to use her brain a whole hell of a lot more than she'd been doing lately. She could only hope that she was still sharp enough after the months of drudgery she'd endured in this lab.

Erin didn't waste any more time. She found a microscope in one of the cabinets, set it up on her desk, then handed her chart to Sean, pointing at the columns on the far right of it. "Can you print out the reports belonging to these four newer IDs, here? And one of the older ones, to compare."

He paused for a moment, watching her. It made her uneasy.

Are you okay?

Erin tried to ignore his question. *I'll be fine once I find something helpful.*

Sean nodded and left her to it.

Time crawled as Erin checked the samples one after the other, taking pictures of each slide before moving on to the next. They couldn't stay here all night, doing this. The longer they remained inside the lab, the more likely they'd get caught.

It was a scary thought, but not enough to make her stop what she was doing.

Professor Blake had involved her in something she wanted nothing to do with. The least she could do was to try and get to the bottom of it all.

It took her about half an hour in all, but she was finally ready. She even took soft copies of all the transcriptions she'd done for the professor, even though the data in them had never made sense to her before.

"We should check his office," Erin said.

Sean nodded in silence. *But not too long.*

Erin agreed. They'd spent way too much time here already.

They rushed out of the lab, and down the hall.

Footsteps, Sean warned, pulling Erin into a doorway.

Her heart skipped a few beats, feeling his body so close to hers. *No, focus!*

Erin held her breath until the threat had passed and they were able to continue on to the professor's office.

It was locked, but that was hardly a deterrent for Sean,

who picked the lock in minutes.

I thought you were a cop? Erin wondered. *Is this legal?*

Not quite, but lives are at stake. We need more evidence.

Erin didn't argue.

Once inside, she went straight for the filing cabinet behind Professor Blake's desk. She was ruthless, undiscerning. Everything he had, every file, every document, she stacked up on his desk and went through, taking pictures of each page before putting the papers back in the same order she'd found them.

Sean followed her example and began doing the same on a stack of papers from inside a desk drawer.

I'm going to need a lot of time to understand all this, Erin thought.

I wish I could help you, Sean responded.

Erin looked up at him and smiled bleakly. *Just get the guy. Make him pay.*

I will.

Time stood still as they looked into each other's eyes. For a moment, Erin forgot everything that had weighed so heavily on her all day. She even forgot how cold he'd acted toward her only minutes earlier.

Neither of them heard the footsteps outside. Or noticed the beam of light filtering through the frosted glass of the door.

Until said door swung open.

They were caught.

CHAPTER TEN

Sean had been so distracted, he didn't notice the impending threat. He hadn't even heard the man approach. Not until he stood in the open doorway, anyway. They were so screwed.

Sean turned around slowly and instinctively positioned himself between Erin and the door. A familiar face awaited him.

"What are you—" Mel, the guard who'd trained Sean and Cooper, did not finish his question.

He stared at the two of them, his mouth agape, focusing on Sean first. Then, Mel leaned to the side to catch a glimpse of Erin.

"Well, this certainly is unexpected. I thought I picked up on a certain vibe between you two the other day. But here? In your boss's office?" That latter remark was clearly aimed at Erin.

Sean cleared his throat. "This isn't what it looks like." Who was he kidding, this was worse than it looked.

"It ain't? Oh well. It looks exciting if you ask me." The sarcasm was dripping off Mel's voice.

"Mel," Erin said softly, pushing her way past Sean. "You've known me for a little while now… You're not going to tell on me, are you?"

Mel folded his arms. "I'm not too fond of your boss,

but what exactly do you expect me to do? I can't imagine you have permission to be here."

Go on, tell him why you're here. He'll have no choice but to help us.

Are you sure we can trust him? Sean turned around and studied Erin's face.

She looked terrified. *We don't really have a choice, do we?*

He wanted to hold her, tell her everything would be alright. Of course, he did nothing of the sort.

Sean turned around again and stared Mel down. *I could take him out. I wouldn't injure him, just enough for us to get away.*

Oh no! Nobody else is getting hurt on my account. The guilt he'd felt emanating from her earlier was back. She seemed to have soft spot for the guard, so incapacitating him was no longer an option.

"Mel. The professor has been working on something really dangerous. Something that could kill thousands," Erin spoke up again.

"You don't say," Mel said.

"Tell him, Sean," Erin pleaded.

Sean took a deep breath. This had to be the worst undercover gig he'd ever been involved in. Two days in, and his cover was completely blown, plus he'd kissed a suspect, before breaking into a possible crime scene with her.

"I haven't been truthful with you," Sean started. "I'm not here to work as a guard."

"I can see that." Mel folded his arms in front of him.

"I'm part of Alpha Squad, a government task force—" he said, flashing his badge.

"I know what Alpha Squad is. You guys investigated that burglary case over in Blackpool recently. I saw it on the news, though I didn't see you in any of the footage. I'm good with faces, I am." Mel's voice had softened, as had his previously stern expression.

"Yeah, that was just before my time. I was still in training," Sean explained.

"Well, what's this all about then?" Mel asked.

"Two shifters have died. We like the professor as a suspect." It was best to keep things vague. "Erin's helping me find out how he did it."

"This true?" Mel asked Erin.

Erin nodded, even in the half-dark, the tears filling her eyes were enough to tear at anyone's heartstrings. Despite everything, she really knew how to play to her strengths.

Mel nodded. "Well as I said, I never liked the guy. If you're onto something here, who am I to stand in your way? Especially since you're on government business."

"Thank you, Mel. You're the best," Erin said.

"Yeah, yeah. But I do like this job, alright? You didn't see me here. I didn't see you. I'm not getting fired over this," Mel insisted.

"I didn't see anybody," Erin agreed.

Sean shook his head in disbelief. A little feminine charm went a long way.

As if. He's a fan of the squad, that's why he's willing to help, Erin disagreed.

"Thanks, mate," Sean said.

"Let me know if you need any help with the guy, okay?" Mel told Erin.

See? Sean rolled his eyes.

"I will," Erin confirmed.

"I trust you'll find your own way out once you're done here," Mel said, as he closed the door behind him.

Sean breathed a sigh of relief. *You really have no idea of the effect you have on people, do you?*

Erin frowned. *What do you mean?*

Sean walked over to the small fridge that stood off to the side of Professor Blake's desk and inspected its contents before settling on a bottle of Evian. This could have very well turned into a disaster.

Nobody, not even the rest of the squad, would have been able to get them out of trouble if Mel had called the police. They didn't even have any evidence worth showing to the local authorities yet. Until Erin was able to make sense of the data they'd taken, they were on their own.

Through his own stupidity and recklessness, he had very nearly gotten Erin into a whole heap of trouble.

"I think this is probably enough," Erin said, as she stuffed all the files she'd photographed back into Professor Blake's filing cabinet.

"Agreed." Eager not to leave behind any evidence of

their presence here, Sean refilled the now empty water bottle from the sink in the professor's attached bathroom and placed it back inside the fridge. "Let's go."

He held out his hand, which Erin took without hesitation. Then they sneaked back down the hall, right past the video surveillance room where Cooper and he had spent way too much time yesterday, and into the reception area.

There were still some people around; researchers who had worked late, perhaps. Thankfully nobody paid any attention to them, allowing them to leave the building without arousing suspicion.

"Let's go back to my place. Figure this stuff out," Erin suggested.

Sean wasn't sure how he might contribute, but he didn't have the heart to refuse.

———◆———

They'd worked through the night, with Erin picking up most of the slack. Sean's role had been more supportive than anything. He'd made sure she had all the caffeine and nourishment she needed, and spent the rest of the time contemplating their relationship in silence.

By morning, she had the beginnings of a theory. Meanwhile, he was more confused than ever about how he felt about the woman.

"So, he's been trying to alter DNA. The earlier reports,

I suspect, are all of human subjects. Professor Blake has tried come up with a way to change one specific marker that differentiates human and shifter DNA. Then, he's taken his findings and done a field test."

Sean nodded. "The blood donation drive."

"Right." Erin pulled up some of the documents she'd photographed in Professor Blake's office. "And these four new subjects were donors that day. I think it's safe to assume Jeremy and Walter are in this group. The other two either didn't get exposed, or they weren't shifters. Or you might have had four deaths on your hand instead of two."

Erin sighed and rubbed her eyes.

"Since whatever delivery mechanism he's employing only affects that one marker, it's completely harmless to humans." Erin looked up from her papers, and suppressed a yawn.

"You should probably take some rest," Sean suggested.

Erin shook her head. "No, we've got to tell people about this!"

"I'll take care of it," Sean reassured her. "I can take your notes and show them to my squad leader."

"What I can't work out is how he's doing it. What's the delivery method?" Erin asked.

"Rome wasn't built in a day. We don't have to have all the answers right away," Sean said. "At least this gives us a start, though."

Erin nodded and sank back into the sofa.

It was obvious that she was exhausted. It had been a long and trying day for both of them.

"I think I'll take a quick nap, then we can go brief your squad leader," Erin mumbled.

Sean smiled and shook his head. She was tenacious, this one.

Without giving it any further thought, he picked her up and carried her into the bedroom.

"At least have a proper sleep," he whispered in her ear.

Her face was calm now; the frown that had been etched into her face all night was fading. This hadn't been easy on her. Ever since she'd found out why Sean was really in Inverness, she'd burdened herself with all this guilt. She'd taken the entire affair very personally indeed.

He lay her down against the pillows and stood and watched for a moment.

Sean had never seen a more beautiful woman in his entire life.

That didn't make their connection any less inappropriate, though. He'd kissed her this afternoon. And all evening, and throughout the night, he'd done his best to keep those same urges locked up deep inside of him. They had work to do. Getting involved with her had been a double-edged sword.

Wildly unethical, but without her, he wouldn't have found all this evidence either.

Sean wasn't sure what to make of it.

Perhaps if they got some distance between them, he

could find some clarity.

But he still found himself here, in her bedroom.

Her deep, calm breaths told him she'd already fallen asleep.

Finally.

He ought to take her final notes and show them to Eric and the rest of the guys immediately. Although he'd obtained this evidence illegally, perhaps it would be enough to get the local authorities involved in the investigation.

If they couldn't prove Professor Blake had killed the two shifters, at the very least they had evidence of an illegal human trial of some sort. If Erin's hypothesis was correct, DNA testing would quickly prove that two of the four new samples belonged to the victims. That would be enough to reopen the investigation and consider alternate causes of death.

But… he couldn't leave her bedside.

He wasn't the sort of guy to spend the night at a woman's house—albeit for work and not pleasure—and then sneak out while she was asleep.

The challenges of the past twelve or so hours were catching up with him as well. He stretched, but still noticed a weird stiffness in his neck and shoulders which he was unaccustomed to.

Perhaps he was just tired as well.

Sean leaned back against the pillows next to Erin, and

brushed a stray lock of hair behind her ear.

His eyelids grew heavy, so he sank down further, resting his arm protectively around her. With his face nestling against her hair, he sank into a deep, dreamless slumber.

———•◆•———

When he awoke, Erin was sitting up in bed, watching him.

"What time is it?" Sean mumbled, rubbing his eyes.

The strain in his shoulders had become worse, and his temples were throbbing. He'd survived many long nights as a detective, and never once felt like this because of it. This fatigue was completely alien to him.

"Just after seven," Erin said. "Are you alright? You look tired."

Sean sat up as well and tried to find his bearings.

How had he allowed this to happen? He'd thrown propriety out the window on this one and fallen asleep in her bed, without even asking for permission first.

I'm so sorry, I shouldn't be here, he thought.

It's okay. After the night we've had, I'm glad I didn't wake up alone.

The sunlight filtering through the curtains was painfully bright. Sean shielded his eyes and turned to face Erin instead.

"I should check in with the squad. They'll be wondering where I've been," he said, and swung his legs out of bed, only to find that his balance was strangely off.

"I think you need more rest," Erin observed.

He felt wobbly on his feet, his coordination severely impaired. Was this what it felt like to be drunk?

"I've never felt like this before," he said.

Erin rushed out of bed and took his hand. "You seem a bit warm. How do you feel?" she asked.

Sean shook his head. "It'll pass, I'm sure."

"You told me shifters don't get sick."

"They—I mean, we, don't, apparently," he mumbled.

"You don't look well to me," Erin whispered.

Sean didn't feel well either. He sat back down on the bed and rubbed a particularly painful spot on the center of his forehead. Any relief he got from that was fleeting.

"Faith!" He heard Erin call out and knock on another door in the house. "Faith, I'm sorry to wake you, but I need your car," she said.

Sean tried to shake off the heaviness in his head, but that just made him dizzy. It was the weirdest thing. The room seemed to spin.

Within minutes, Erin was back carrying a bunch of keys.

"Come on," she said, guiding him back onto his feet. "You need to tell me where the rest of your squad is. We're going in together, right now!"

Sean nodded, then held his head when the spinning sensation got worse.

"Okay."

"Whatever this is, it's not good," Erin whispered. "Not good at all."

Sean wasn't sure how he made it downstairs, and into the passenger seat of the faded red Suzuki parked outside. He mumbled a few directions while Erin navigated the empty streets, until they reached the centrally located guest house the squad had booked.

He couldn't muster the energy to get out, so he sat back, with his eyes closed.

There was a period of pure blackness, before he found himself in a clean bed with white, crisp sheets, and a group of concerned looking faces hovering above him.

"So you think he's been exposed?" Eric's voice asked.

Was he imagining things? Where was he? Sean tried to get up, but someone rested their hand heavily on his shoulder.

You need to rest, Erin's voice infiltrated his mind. *You're at the hospital.*

He opened his eyes again and let his gaze settle on her face. She was here.

"It's the only explanation," she told Eric. "We went into Professor Blake's office—my boss's office—together, and now, he's sick."

"How do we know you didn't infect him?" Cooper's face came into view.

Sean balled his fists. *How dare he accuse her of something so heinous?*

It's okay, he doesn't know.

Eric made a calming gesture. "I think I can see what's going on here." He made eye contact with Sean. "She's not at fault."

Sean closed his eyes and tried to breathe, but something was constricting his chest.

"I'm not sure she should be here," Cooper added.

Sean tried to protest, but he was unable to speak. A tickle in the back of his throat caused his chest to spasm. The resulting noise was hideous. So that was what it felt like to cough.

"Okay, everybody out! Let the doctor do his stuff," Eric ordered. "Meanwhile, Major Williams will be here later today, so let's be ready to brief her about the case so far."

Don't go, Sean pleaded.

Erin pulled her chair closer and placed her hand on Sean's arm. *I won't leave you. But he won't get away with this. I'll find a cure, if it's the last thing I do.*

That was the last thing Sean remembered.

CHAPTER ELEVEN

It hadn't been easy, leaving Sean's bedside. But without knowing exactly what he was suffering from, there was no way of fighting it. She wasn't in the habit of feeling helpless.

"Are you sure you're ready for this?" Eric King—the man Sean had pointed out as his superior on the squad—said.

Erin nodded. As ready as she was ever going to be.

"We'll be standing by. Try to get him to admit to it."

I won't just get the professor to confess, I'm going to get a cure, Erin told herself. She had to. For Sean's sake.

Sean's commander shook her hand, and sent her on her way.

Erin hurried to work, ready to take a stand. How hard could it be? If she'd learned anything about the man these past couple of months it was that he had trouble filtering his words when he got riled up. It wouldn't be difficult to push his buttons. If only she could keep her cool long enough to steer the conversation where she needed it to go…

The lab was empty except for Glenn, so she retreated into the hallway. She hoped beyond hope that Blake was in his office.

He was the only one who could help now. And by

God, she wasn't sure how far she was prepared to go if he was unwilling.

She marched down the hall, phone in hand, trying her best to keep her emotions in check, but it was no use.

By the time she pushed the door to his office open, tears were stinging in her eyes.

Thankfully, there he was, sitting behind his desk. She quickly dialed Eric King's number and slipped the phone into her pocket, just as he'd instructed. *This better work!*

Professor Blake looked up, sporting the usual disapproving frown he reserved for his lab minions.

"Erin! Where have you been all morning? And don't you know to knock before—"

Erin shook her head. "I don't care. This ends now."

"What are you—"

She approached his desk and leaned across it with both her palms resting flat on top of its wooden surface. If the situation wasn't so dead serious, the scene might have been comical. She was giving him her best bad cop impression, only, she wasn't faking her anger.

"You're going to tell me what you've been up to right now. People have died! People are still—" She couldn't finish that sentence. The thought of Sean succumbing to the same thing that had killed Jeremy and the other man, Walter, stung too much.

The professor sat back in his chair. "So, you know."

He folded his hands in his lap and studied her for a

moment, before starting one of his usual lectures.

"You've always been too clever for your own good, Erin. I knew it the moment I interviewed you. But I gave you a chance anyway, didn't I?"

She slammed her hand down hard on the desk.

"What did you give these people? Is it a pathogen of some sort? I need to know right now!" Erin demanded.

The professor smiled bleakly. "You have no idea what you're talking about."

"You killed two people. Who knows how many you infected in the first place."

"During a project of this scale, there are bound to be casualties," Professor Blake explained in a tone so artificially calm it sounded downright patronizing. "Plus, live subjects are hard to come by."

"That's where you're going to take this?" she asked. *He's gone mad.*

"It's like curing any other disease, don't you see? It's only natural for there to be some side effects."

"Death is merely a side effect to you." Erin couldn't believe what she was hearing.

He shook his head. "Well it wasn't the aim, I can assure you."

The man spoke as though he was curing cancer or something. It took everything for her not to lose her cool completely.

"Just the other night you had that maniac, Victor Domnall, in your office here with you. Don't you lecture me about what your goal was. I'm pretty sure *his* aims have been met perfectly."

The professor sighed. "I know how it looks, but trust me, there was merit in his proposal."

"His proposal? To what, kill all shifters? Starting with a couple of completely innocent ones who volunteered to donate their blood in order to help people?" Erin was shaking with rage.

He shook his head. "No, you silly child. To cure them!"

She opened her mouth to protest, but it took her a moment to find the right words.

"But… they're not sick!"

"How would you know? They randomly morph into fantastical creatures, sometimes without even wanting to. They're not normal either, are they? I'm sure they'll flock to me in droves, volunteering to take my cure. Once I get it exactly right, of course."

Erin straightened herself and balled her fists, then released them again. He'd lost his mind.

Taking a deep breath, she spoke as calmly as she could. "I need to know how to counter it. Whatever this supposed cure is that you've been testing, it's not working. I need to—"

The professor leaned forward shand picked up a bottle of Evian water from his desk, unscrewing the cap. "Has someone come into contact with something they shouldn't have? Perhaps someone you care about?" He took a sip, while continuing to maintain eye contact with Erin.

Bloody hell. This was how Sean had become infected. Assuming the supposed 'cure' the professor had been working on wasn't airborne, the only unusual thing Sean had done while they snooped around the lab and this office was have a sip of water.

The professor was testing the effects on humans on himself. Live subjects were hard to come by, in his own words.

And that's how he'd done it at the blood donation drive as well. The refreshments!

If looks could kill, Erin's would have done a fine job at it. She snatched the bottle out of Blake's hands and screwed the cap back on tightly. This was evidence. She wouldn't let it out of her sight until she had a look at a sample of it under a microscope.

"Not everyone is a research subject." Her throat felt tight, like it was closing up. Never in her life had she feared for someone like this. And she was well acquainted with loss, perhaps even somewhat desensitized to it, ever since the tragic death of her parents.

But she couldn't face the thought of losing Sean. Despite only meeting for the first time a couple of days ago, he'd made a big impression on her. They could hear each other's thoughts, for heaven's sake. She knew in her heart that she'd never meet anyone else like him.

She'd never love another.

And she hadn't even had the chance to tell him as

much.

"Well, in that case, I have some bad news for you." The professor's expression was solemn as he leaned back in his chair again.

Erin pressed her lips together. *No. Don't you say it!*

"There is no antidote. At least not that I know of. Of course, I was never looking for one…"

His words were like a punch in the gut. She felt her knees buckle underneath her, but caught herself at the last moment, leaning once again against the desk.

"No. I don't believe it," she whispered.

"I'm sorry, child. I cannot help you."

"You have no concept of what you've done." Erin looked up. Her eyes narrowed as she glared at him through her tears.

The professor shrugged awkwardly. Perhaps it was something in the way she looked at him that had suddenly made him uneasy.

She'd never been a violent person, but right this moment, she felt capable of anything.

To avenge Sean, there was no limit to what she would do. Just as soon as the professor proved himself completely useless to her cause, she'd make him understand the pain he'd caused. She would make him suffer like she suffered.

"Look, I have somewhere to be," the professor mumbled, pushing his chair back and attempting to get up.

"So, if you will excuse me."

Erin shook her head and pointed at him. "You're not going anywhere."

He pressed his lips together and watched as she took her phone out of her pocket and raised it to her ear. "Did you get all that?"

"Yes, good work." Eric King had been standing by on the other end of the line all along. Just as they'd agreed.

The professor scoffed and was about to say something, but she snapped her finger and gave him a stern look, silencing him. The tables were turned now. Underneath all the self-importance and arrogance, Blake was just a coward.

"We'll be right over with the local police. Don't let him leave," Sean's squad leader said.

"Don't worry. I won't." Erin cut the call and put the phone back in her pocket.

If he wanted to, he'd have no problem overpowering her.

She stood barely five foot five whereas he was closer to six feet tall. But she wasn't intimidated by him. She was fueled by rage, by fear of what was going to happen to Sean.

Adrenaline was coursing through her body. Right at this moment, she could move mountains to get what she wanted.

She sat down across from him and crossed her legs.

"Now, why don't you tell me who all was involved?"

she asked. "Did Glenn know?"

The professor shook his head. "I don't have to tell you anything. You can't even keep me here. Don't you see, you've played all your cards already? The next phase of my experiment has already begun and neither you nor whoever is on the other end of that phone can change it."

Now what was that supposed to mean?

He reached for the phone on his desk and dialed a number. Erin just watched him, unimpressed. It had to be a bluff, his final attempt to get her to back off.

She was not about to fall for that.

"Security? I have a situation in my office that needs dealing with," Blake said, while keeping his eyes fixed on her.

Erin just smirked at him. *As if.*

Barely a minute later, a knock on the door interrupted the loaded silence between them.

"Come in," Professor Blake barked. His voice was higher pitched than normal. It was obvious that he was tense.

Erin didn't even turn around in her chair. She already knew who would have gotten the call.

"Professor Blake. What seems to be the problem?" Mel's jovial voice filled the whole room. If Erin didn't feel so desperate, it would have been enough to make her smile. But instead, she kept glaring at the professor, who did his best to avoid her gaze.

"I need you to escort this young lady out. She's been fired." The professor's expression turned smug. Erin scoffed and shook her head. *That's not going to last.*

"Erin?" Mel addressed her.

Erin turned around to face him. "We've got him, Mel. He can't wiggle his way out anymore," she whispered.

"Well?" the professor asked. "Take her away!"

"I'm afraid I can't do that," Mel said.

"Do you want me to go to your supervisor and tell him you're refusing to do your job here? What's your name?" Blake demanded.

"Make sure he doesn't leave," Erin said as she got up, carrying the water bottle she'd confiscated as evidence. "The police are on their way. He's got a lot to answer for."

She'd wasted enough time already. If Sean was awake, he would be wondering where she was.

No matter what, she wanted to have as much time with him as possible.

"Sure thing, love. He's going nowhere." Mel winked at her as she passed him. "Give my best to McMillan. He seems like a good lad. I would have liked to work with him some more."

Erin considered her answer. She didn't have the heart to tell Mel what had happened. "Thanks. Will do."

She rushed out the door, down the hall, and across the reception area. Although she was quite aware this was probably the last time she'd set foot in the health center, she felt no nostalgia toward it. She had more important places to be. She might not have been able to get an antidote, but she wasn't ready to completely give up yet either. She still had that water bottle, and whatever was left inside. If she could figure out what was in it, perhaps she could figure out how to help Sean.

Once outside, she unlocked Faith's car and was just about to get in, when she felt a presence. She was being watched.

She tried to turn around, but before she had the chance to see her assailant, a sharp, blinding pain passed through the back of her neck through her head. She dropped the keys and Evian bottle to the ground and everything went black.

The last thing that went through her mind was just a single, basic thought: would she ever see Sean again?

CHAPTER TWELVE

When Sean woke up, he was completely alone. The chair where Erin had sat before he'd fallen asleep was empty.

The door to his room was closed, but he could hear muffled voices elsewhere in the building.

He was in pain. Real, stabbing pain, like every bone in his body had been broken.

But that wasn't the worst of it. *Where's Erin?*

She wouldn't just leave him after promising she'd stay?

What an idiot he'd been, anyway. He'd been fighting his attraction to her. Rejecting the thought of a relationship with her because of rules that seemed utterly trivial now.

He'd obviously been infected with the same thing that had killed the other two victims.

He was going to die right here, in this bed.

Nothing brought more clarity than foreseeing your own demise.

He should have never tried to distance himself from her. Maybe if he'd been less of an ass about everything, she'd still be sitting there, at his bedside.

Unless…

"Hello?" he called out, then was immediately rendered helpless by a fresh coughing fit. His lungs were on fire.

Was this what it felt like to be fully human? He'd seen his mother down with a flu or cold, and he could never quite relate to what that was like. Of course, he himself had never so much as suffered from a runny nose.

Shifters don't get sick, as Adam had said during their first briefing about this case.

Footsteps approached, and Sean forced himself up in his bed. His muscles barely wanted to cooperate. So this was what it was like to feel weak, and so very tired.

"McMillan, you really ought to rest," Cooper said as he peeped inside the room.

"Where's Erin?" Sean had to force the words out in between further coughs.

"She'll be right back, I'm sure... Look, this isn't your problem. Let us take care of it, won't you?"

Sean pulled at the sheet that covered him and struggled to swing his legs out of bed so that he could get up.

Cooper was on him within a split second, pushing him backwards against the pillows.

"I can't just lie here, while who knows what is going on out there! Don't you get it?" Sean protested.

"You're not well. At least get better first!" Cooper argued, while continuing to keep him pinned down by his shoulder. They exchanged a quick look. Cooper's expression was somber; although he'd tried to put on a brave face, he knew very well Sean wasn't getting better anytime soon.

Ordinarily Sean was at least twice, if not thrice as strong as the man, but not today. It was pointless to struggle further. Sean closed his eyes and tried to take a deep breath, which only resulted in another terrible, itchy rattle deep in his chest.

He coughed some more, but it seemed to not make much of a difference. It was hard to breathe. If he couldn't even get air, what hope was there that he could even stand up?

"Will you at least be straight with me? Where is she?"

"Last I saw her, she was talking to Eric," Cooper said.

"Okay, when was that?"

"That's got to be an hour or so ago now."

"Then why isn't she back?"

"Look, mate. I don't know. You think he tells me anything?" Cooper complained. "We're just waiting on the major now. She left the base as soon as she found out about what happened to you. We'll have a plan of action in place soon enough."

Something was very wrong, and they weren't telling him. Why would they? Sean wasn't one of them. He was just some latecomer to the shifter taskforce party. He shouldn't even have joined the squad in the first place.

And he shouldn't have dragged Erin into this either.

"Will you tell her to see me if you find her? Erin, I mean," he said under his breath. It was all the volume he could manage without choking on whatever had filled up his lungs.

"Sure thing, mate. Don't worry." Cooper forced a smile and left his bedside. He obviously couldn't wait to get out of the room.

Before Sean knew it, the door had shut behind Cooper, and he was alone again.

He closed his eyes and focused on keeping calm. But his heart was racing, and his head was pounding. All the veins on the side of his head seemed ready to pop. How was he meant to think with a headache like this? Weren't there medicines for this sort of thing?

He vaguely remembered a doctor being present when Erin had brought him in, but if he'd even done anything at all to help, it hadn't done him much good.

Sean slid down in his bed and tried to get a little more comfortable. It felt like he was nodding along with every heartbeat. Or perhaps he was just imagining that.

His thoughts continued to stay with Erin. He couldn't feel her anymore. She wasn't in the building for sure. What could be so bloody important that she'd leave him here all alone?

Sean jerked up, his eyes wide open, when he realized exactly what it could be.

The last thing she'd said to him. *He's not going to get away with this. I'll find a cure, if it's the last thing I do.* His memories were fuzzy, but he was pretty sure he hadn't imagined that.

She'd gone to confront the professor to get information out of him. Probably with Eric's blessing. And she hadn't yet come back.

That was why they weren't telling him anything.

They'd let her out of here and walk right into the lion's den, no matter the consequences. What if she got hurt, or worse? He wouldn't be able to forgive them. Or himself.

Sean's body quivered and trembled, as fur fought to emerge from his skin and claws tried to break through his fingers and toes. It was impossible. It was like his human form was frozen solid and his animal could no longer break free.

He lay back in the pillows, panting helplessly. There was no way he could get up and help her.

Sean inhaled deeply and let out a roar loud enough it made the windows rattle.

The punishment for his exertion was immediate. His eyes grew heavy and a heavy blanket of darkness descended over him as he was pulled into a restless, nightmare laden slumber.

———◆———

Sean awoke to the sound of a female voice. It wasn't Erin, though. He would have known instantly. No matter how deep the dream he found himself in, he was certain he'd sense her presence.

"What's the prognosis?" Major Williams asked.

"We're not quite sure, major," someone else said.

"Well, are the symptoms the same?" the major demanded.

Footsteps approached.

"Janine, we have no way of knowing. Walter Perth's family never noticed when he got sick. Neither did the other victim's friends. But by all accounts the others were fine for a couple of days at least, whereas McMillan was affected within hours of his exposure." This second male voice was even more familiar.

Sean opened his eyes and blinked against the harsh light overhead until he could finally focus on the unexpected company in his room.

Eric, who stood by Major Williams's side was the first to notice he'd woken up, and gestured at the attending doctor to come closer.

"He's awake," Eric whispered.

"Sean," Eric addressed him in a louder voice. "How are you feeling?"

How was he feeling? He blinked again and reached for his forehead. The remnants of the pounding headache he'd suffered from earlier were still blurring his vision.

Sean shook his head. "Where's Erin?"

Major Williams shot Eric a questioning look. He returned her gaze and stared at her for a moment. Her expression relaxed again and she nodded.

He'd called her Janine just now, Sean remembered. There definitely *was* something going on between them.

But such trivial observations weren't enough to distract him. He had just one question on his mind and he'd be damned if he wouldn't get the answer.

"Bloody hell, where's Erin?" he bellowed.

Eric raised his hand in a calming gesture and approached him. "You should relax. You're not well."

"I need to know. And I feel fine!" Sean sat up in bed to make his point.

He really did feel much better.

His body still ached all over, but it was nothing like the blinding pain he'd felt before. In any case, it wasn't his own well-being he was worried about.

The major's face lit up. "Doctor, if you would check the patient's vitals, please."

"His temperature is down, as is his heartbeat. I'd have to take his blood to comment on anything further."

Sean frowned. Why was nobody listening to him?

"I just said I feel fine."

"What medicines have you given him? Whatever it was must have worked," the major asked. "We should take note, so we can employ the same sort of treatment in future."

Again, they were talking about him like he wasn't even there.

The doctor scratched his head and double-checked Sean's chart. "Well that's the thing. We didn't want to risk making things worse by giving him the wrong medication, so he's just been on a saline drip, that's all. These improvements, they're all him."

Sean shook his head. They were testing his patience.

He threw the covers off and pulled the needle out of

his arm.

"Whoa, mate. Calm down!" Eric protested.

Sean shot him a nasty glare. "You let her go back to the clinic, didn't you? To talk to the professor?"

"How did you—" Eric didn't finish the question and took a step back with both his hands held up. "She did well, your girl. Got him to admit everything on tape. The police have already brought in the suspect."

Sean shook his head. "Then why hasn't she come back? Something must have happened to her."

That was it; that was the discomfort he felt. The after-effects of his mysterious disease aside, he was fearing for her safety. In her presence, he'd been able to sense her emotions, hear her thoughts. In her absence, he felt that she was in danger.

Of course she'd gone in of her own accord; probably felt it was the only thing she could do to fix what had happened. He was still furious with Eric for letting her leave without back-up, but there was no time to dwell on that. They had to act, right now.

"We have to go get her," Sean concluded.

Eric nodded, and exchanged another look with the major, who had so far just stood by in silence.

"Let's track her movements. Who last saw her, that sort of thing," Sean said. "Wait, I know just who can help."

He reached for his pocket, only to find that he was wearing a weird pajama type thing. "Where's my phone?"

"Are you sure you're alright?" Major Williams asked.

Sean nodded. "I'll feel a lot better once we get Erin back."

She picked up his mobile from the bedside table and handed it over, all the while making eye contact with him. "I understand. Shifters mate for life," she said, in the most matter-of-fact tone.

Sean frowned. What had she just said?

"But before you leave this room, the doctor will draw your blood and perform any test he wants, is that clear?" she added.

That was fair. Sean nodded and focused on the task at hand. He had to talk to Mel. The man had little loyalty for him, but for Erin, he'd be happy to help. If he reviewed any camera footage of the health center premises from the past hour or so, perhaps it would reveal where Erin had gone and what had happened to her.

CHAPTER THIRTEEN

Erin woke up with a dull headache, extending all the way from the back of her head around toward her temples. She opened her eyes, briefly, but had trouble identifying her surroundings in the dark.

A couple of voices and corresponding footsteps approached. She stayed absolutely still and just listened.

"Looks like she's still out," one of the strangers observed.

Good, that was what she wanted them to think.

"We can't just leave her here, can we?" the other asked.

"Why not? Victor said to travel light."

So she'd been caught by Victor Domnall's men! That made sense.

"Well, what do we do with her? Did he tell you to kill her?"

Erin's heart sank. She wasn't ready to die, not without seeing Sean one last time and telling him exactly what he meant to her.

"She's a witness. We don't leave witnesses."

"She ain't seen our faces. Shifter scum, I don't mind, but she's one of us, mate!"

The two continued to argue back and forth for a bit. Erin tried to keep listening, but she was having trouble accepting her desperate fate. Perhaps she ought to try fighting back.

She tried to move her arms, but found that her wrists had been tied together. The best she could hope for was if they decided to just leave her here to die.

Perhaps someone would find her just in time, even if she had no idea where she was.

Erin tried to listen for sounds that might tell her where she was. There was nothing specific she could latch onto. Just road noise.

This place had to be close to a big road. Not that this one detail helped narrow things down for her. She didn't even know how long she'd been out for and how far they drove to get here.

Erin took a deep breath and tried not to lose hope completely.

"Do you know if the others made it to the water treatment place?"

Erin's ears perked up. *They're not serious!*

"Last I heard everything was set."

"Why couldn't we have been put on that job? There would've been some glory in that at least. Instead we're stuck here, playing second fiddle as usual."

"Stop complaining, will you? Bloody hell, you're like an old hag. If Victor thought you were ready for that kind of responsibility, he'd assign you accordingly."

"Look who's talking. I'm not the only one stuck in this godforsaken place, babysitting some random girl."

"You're an idiot."

Erin sighed. If the bickering didn't stop soon, she'd lose her cool with these two clowns herself. Consequences be damned.

Actually, perhaps she could buy herself some time by pitching these two against each other some more.

"Anyway, why don't we finish her off now, so we're ready to go when Victor calls."

Erin held her breath. There was no time to lose.

"What the hell?" she called out, struggling to sit up straight. "Where's Victor?"

"What did she say?" one of the men whispered. "Did she just ask for Victor?"

She squinted and scanned the room. It was too dark for her to recognize the two men's faces; they were just silhouettes in the shadows.

"Don't listen to her. It's got to be a trick."

"You idiots!" Erin shouted. "You were supposed to capture the other girl, not me! I was there to get the toxin from the professor and deliver it to Victor!"

"Bloody hell, she knows about the plan."

"Of course I know about the plan. I'm one of you!" she raged.

Her heart was racing even faster now. Would they buy it? If they called Victor Domnall to confirm, she was done for.

One of the guys approached until she could finally see him more clearly. He looked about thirty, with a shaved head that showed some shading around the temples. His lanky physique was clad entirely in camo, with his baggy cargoes stuffed into the tops of black lace-up boots. He was a walking, talking cliché.

The other man, who seemed to be in his forties, came up to her as well. There was nothing unusual about him; he seemed completely ordinary. The family man next door, or the stuffy office worker who you wouldn't remember if he sat next to you on the bus.

"If you're really one of us, then what's the password?" he asked.

Erin pressed her lips together. *Crap!*

"I thought as much." The older guy turned away again.

"No, wait!" Erin called out.

"Yes?"

She took a deep breath. This was it. Her final stand.

"There is no password. What do you think, I'm some kind of ditzy bimbo who's going to be impressed by all this?" she shouted.

The younger one of her captors looked utterly shocked, while the older one smiled briefly and shook his head.

"Sorry, love. This isn't going to work out," the latter said.

"Mate, I don't think—"

"You shut up and do as you're told, alright? Kill her. Leave her here. I'm gonna go get rid of the car."

Erin closed her eyes. That was that then. She was doomed.

Mel had come through.

In the twenty minutes or so it took Alpha Squad to assemble at the health center, the security guard had sifted through some of the surveillance footage and found that one of the parking lot cameras had caught the entire incident on tape.

Erin had been abducted.

After allowing Erin's presence to distract him through almost the entire investigation, Sean had regained his focus. To find her, he would move mountains if he had to.

Right now, though, he was delegating various jobs to the rest of the squad, as well as involving local police in their search effort.

The footage Mel found had captured two masked men, who'd knocked Erin over the back of the head with a small hand-held weapon that looked like a hotel keyring, before stuffing her into the back of Faith's car. Then, they'd simply driven away with her.

The Scotland Police officers who'd already been briefed about Professor Blake's case by Major Williams were helpful enough to check traffic cameras in the surrounding area, and so, they were able to get a rough idea of which direction Erin's captors had fled in.

Sean tried to pull out all the stops to get to her. Tracing her phone didn't get them anywhere, since the abductors had dumped it just down the road from the health center.

"They'd want to take her somewhere private, someplace where nobody could hear her call for help," Sean said.

"There's plenty of open countryside around. They could have gone anywhere," Cooper observed.

Sean shook his head. "It's tourist season. Two dubious looking men driving an old pink car with an incapacitated woman in the back... I don't think they'd take the risk to travel on any of the scenic routes."

"So you think they're still in town somewhere?" Eric asked.

He was still fearing for her safety, of course, but Sean was also in his element. This was the sort of thing he was good at. If anyone could find her, it was him.

"Maybe... I'd be surprised if they risked a long drive. Any industrial complexes or suitable hiding places around the way they headed, south-east from the clinic?" he asked.

One of the uniformed police sent in by the locals cleared his throat. "There's an old storage facility just off the A9 just beyond Bogbain. It's hardly ten minutes from here."

Sean nodded. "Do you have any cameras along the A9?"

The policeman shook his head. "Only in town."

That wasn't much to go on, but it was better than nothing.

"Okay. Are there any more places you can think of?"

Sean asked.

The man thought for a moment, then mentioned a few more locations in the area.

"We'll have to split up to cover more ground," Sean concluded.

He wanted to be the one to find her, obviously, so he had to follow his gut. If he'd learned anything from his short time with Erin, it was to trust his instincts. The policeman's first suggestion felt right.

The squad, accompanied by a handful of policemen and women, soon split into four groups, and began their search.

Sean found himself in the passenger seat of a local police car racing down the A9 with sirens blaring.

"Let's turn those off, so they don't hear us coming," he suggested.

The man nodded and flipped a switch on the car's dashboard.

Sean closed his eyes and focused for a moment. It was as though he could feel her already. They were getting close.

"This is it." Sean opened his eyes as the car slowed down and turned off the A9 and into an unpaved access road.

"How do you kn—" Sean's companion did not get the chance to finish his question.

Up ahead, standing proudly in the center of an

overgrown lot surrounded by a cluster of warehouses, Faith's car was already waiting for them. Erin wasn't in it anymore; Sean could sense her presence deeper inside the compound.

The man in the driver's seat of the old Suzuki looked up and noticed the approaching police car. He started the engine and sped off, as fast as the old car was willing to go.

"You take him, I'm going in to find Erin," Sean said. He didn't wait for an answer, just opened his door and threw himself out onto the cracked concrete, rolling over a few times to soften his fall.

The police car sped off in pursuit of the abductor in Faith's car.

Sean jumped up and sprinted straight ahead, entering the warehouse right in front of him. She was in here—he could feel it—and she was afraid. If he had to fight his way through a thousand men to get to her, he was ready. Erin wouldn't be harmed as long as he was alive.

As it turned out, there was only one man guarding her.

One solitary skinhead with a dazed expression on his face, who barely saw Sean's fist coming before it hit him squarely in the jaw. The man went down without a struggle.

Erin sat further back in the darker part of the warehouse, on top of an old shipping crate with her hands tied in front of her.

Erin's eyes were fixed on his; despite the subdued lighting, he could see her clear as day.

You're here. I don't believe it.

Sean smiled at her, then kneeled beside the man he'd just disabled and swiftly cuffed him.

I couldn't let them hurt you, could I?

Erin took a couple of wobbly steps in his direction, trembling visibly. *But how? How did they cure you?*

Sean shook his head. *They didn't; it went away on its own. The doctor said something about a raised white blood cell count.* In truth, Sean had no idea how he'd recovered and he wasn't in a mood to question it right now.

He'd found her. She was shaken after her ordeal, but she was safe. That was all that mattered.

He rushed toward her and undid her restraints, before wrapping his arms around her. It hadn't been long since they'd been separated; not really. But it had felt like a lifetime.

Let me take you home.

Erin shook her head, though, and pushed away from him. Her eyes were wide with worry as she looked up at him.

"These people, they were planning something. I overheard them," she said.

"Let the police handle it. You've been through enough."

"There's no time to lose. You got infected when you drank the water from the professor's fridge. It's the water, don't you see!"

Sean frowned and shook his head. *I'm going to need more than that.*

"They're planning to infect the entire water supply. They said Victor Domnall's overseeing things himself."

Sean's heart skipped a few beats. If this information was correct, that meant the Sons were ready to take their poison wide. With a current survival rate of 1 in 3, who knew the damage they'd do.

He pulled his phone out of his pocket and dialed Eric.

"We have a problem," Sean started. It didn't take long to explain everything Erin had just told him.

He cut the call, just in time to catch Erin, whose knees were about to buckle. He remembered seeing those men knock her out in the video footage of the clinic parking lot. There was a visible bump on the back of her head. Anger and fear filled his heart when he realized the pain she must be in.

Barely twelve hours after she'd done something similar for him, he carefully carried her to the police car that awaited outside, and raced her to hospital.

CHAPTER FOURTEEN

Erin couldn't help but feel weird as she arrived at the hospital just opposite her former workplace. She was a patient now. She would have never agreed to it normally. But Sean had been so concerned for her once he'd rescued her from that dingy old warehouse, that she didn't have the heart to argue with him.

So here she was, stuck in a room in the Accident & Emergency department, awaiting the results from the CAT scan they'd done on her soon after she'd been admitted.

So much had happened these past couple of days, she'd hardly had the time to reflect. Through the dull headache and occasional bouts of dizziness, her brain was still trying to play catch-up.

Her unexpected reunion with Sean had been a whirlwind of emotions. Where was he, anyway?

How she'd feared for him and tried to prepare herself for the worst. But he'd made it, and come for her.

She still couldn't work out how he'd beaten what everyone had just assumed to be a death sentence courtesy of Professor Blake. Not that she wasn't pleased; she was over the moon, of course.

But her curiosity wasn't letting up either. It was in her nature to want answers and explanations.

And even more pressingly, Erin couldn't stop worrying

about Victor Domnall's plan to infect the town's water supply. She could only hope that Eric and the rest of the squad had arrived in time to stop the threat. How many more would fall sick and die otherwise?

While the doctors at the Accidents & Emergency department had kept her aside for observation, Erin's mind was unable to find rest.

She'd overheard a lot of partial conversations while she'd been at Sean's bedside earlier. The other victims never got sick, or at least nobody was around to notice it.

As far as everyone knew, Jeremy and the other guy showed no symptoms until they suddenly dropped dead almost forty-eight hours after their suspected exposure at the blood donation drive.

Sean, however, had become sick within hours. And just hours after that, he'd miraculously recovered.

Assuming all three were exposed to the same thing, why had his body reacted so differently? Was it down to the level of exposure? Or did he possess some kind of immunity toward it?

If the threat had spread, they'd have to find the answers to these questions as quickly as possible. Lives hung in the balance.

Erin jumped up when the door to her observation room swung open, revealing the one person in the world she wanted to see the most.

"Sean!" she called out. "Did they get him? Please tell me they got him!"

Sean shook his head. *I haven't heard from Eric yet.*

"You really should try to take it easy," he said.

His tone was gentle, caring. Erin closed her eyes and took a deep breath.

How was she meant to calm down when the worst was yet to come?

It'll be okay, don't worry, Sean attempted to comfort her.

She didn't believe it, but it was sweet for him to try, anyway.

One of the doctors who'd examined her earlier also stepped into the room.

"You have a mild concussion, so it's important you rest for a few days."

Erin nodded carefully, in an attempt not to make her dizziness worse.

"Thank you, doctor. I can go, then?"

"Are you sure that's wise? Shouldn't she be kept for observation, or something?" Sean argued.

Erin cocked her head to the side and smiled at him. "He said *mild* concussion. I'll be fine."

And there's no way I'm sitting idle while Victor Domnall is still in the wind.

As it turned out, Erin need not have worried. By the time she'd changed out of the funny robe they'd put her in and left the hospital by Sean's side, his phone rang.

"Eric," he whispered.

Erin squeezed his hand as he answered. With her eyes

closed to maintain focus, she could hear the entire conversation—both sides of it—in her head. By whatever strange magic, she and Sean had become one.

We got there just in time. Victor Domnall and four of his men are in custody right now.

"Great job. So it's finally over," Sean said.

Thanks to your tip, yeah. We got him, and all the evidence necessary to put him away for life.

Erin opened her eyes, finding them moist once again. But these were not tears of sorrow, or fear. Victor Domnall had been caught. The danger was over.

Even though she'd unwittingly played a role in Jeremy and Walter's deaths, she'd been able to prevent further disaster.

She felt light. The weight she'd carried, all that guilt, it had been replaced by relief.

Sean hung up and gave her one of those intense looks he did so well.

"Now that that's out of the way, let's go somewhere quiet. I have a few things I want to say," he said.

Erin studied his face.

In any other relationship, with any other man, a statement like this would fill her heart with dread. But she *knew* him somehow. Whatever he wanted to say, it wasn't bad news.

"My place?" she asked.

———— ◆ ————

Sean had been quiet all the way home. That changed as soon as the door shut behind Erin and him.

"I owe you an apology," he started.

Erin frowned. "What for?"

"It wasn't right, how I acted with you. I could say it's because I was confused. I didn't know how to deal with all these emotions…"

Erin bit her lip and took his hand. His touch affected her more now than ever.

Every meeting, every moment together, had only intensified her feelings for him. She was changed, for the better.

"I don't know what you mean," she said.

"I shouldn't have kissed you when I did. And then I shouldn't have been so cold toward you back at the lab. I realize that now."

Erin smiled at him and took his hands, leading him to the couch in the living room.

"But this is confusing. I've never felt like this before either."

"You'd asked me yesterday, if it was a weird shifter thing," Sean said.

"Yeah?"

"I didn't know it then, but yes. My team mates pretty much confirmed it."

"Confirmed what?"

"Shifters mate for life," Sean whispered.

Erin forgot to breathe. She'd known it, deep inside. She'd already felt that their bond was unshakable, despite hardly knowing him. But to hear Sean say it, in that deep, sexy voice of his, was a whole other matter.

She sank down onto the sofa, and Sean joined her, resting his hand on her thigh.

Her skin grew warm under his touch. What would it be like to go further? To celebrate their union on a more carnal level?

I want that too. But I still have so much to say.

So tell me.

Sean cupped her face, and leaned over to kiss her. His lips were so gentle, yet full of hungry passion, it brought tears to her eyes.

I'm not like the other guys, Sean thought.

I knew that from the first moment we met. Erin stared into his eyes. Every time she looked at him, it was like there was something different, some new truth to discover.

I mean like other shifters also. I've never been one of them. I've always lived between two worlds. Not fully human and not quite shifter either.

Erin's eyes widened. He was a hybrid! That made so much sense. His weird reaction the other day when she'd just assumed he was a shifter. His slip-ups when he spoke about shifter traits, seemingly distancing himself from them.

It even explained why his body had reacted so differently. Why he'd been able to fight Professor Blake's failed attempt at gene therapy and recovered so quickly.

You're different. Unique.

Sean nodded. *Never wanted to be, but yes.*

I think that's beautiful. Who wants to be exactly like everyone else?

Sean smiled briefly. *Trouble is, I don't know exactly how any of this really works. It's all new to me.*

Erin wrapped her arms around him and pulled him against her again.

Nobody knows how love works. We'll figure it out for ourselves.

Promise? Sean seemed to ask.

Of course. I'm never letting you go now. Erin sealed her promise with another kiss. And another.

Words suddenly seemed meaningless and inadequate. If they were to show each other how they truly felt, they had to do it physically. Let instinct take over.

As it turned out, shifters were good at that. Even hybrids, like Sean.

If someone had told Erin three days ago she'd meet a guy and fall into bed with him that same week, she would have argued 'til the cows came home. She wasn't that kind of girl. Her past relationships were of the slow and steady variety. Sense and logic had always prevailed.

Of course, she'd never felt like this before.

She'd never felt this fire in her heart, that would manage to brighten even the darkest of days. This uncontrollable desire to give herself to another, without a single concern for the consequences.

But she was a fast learner.

"Not here," she mumbled, and slipped out of Sean's embrace.

Ready to cast off all restraints from her past life, her past choices, she started to undress. T-shirt, jeans, even underwear; she littered the floor on the way to her bedroom with all of it.

Sean followed, catching up with her right in front of her bed.

She stood naked in front of him, literally and figuratively. She had nothing to hide.

He sank to his knees in front of her and wrapped his arms around her thighs, pulling her against him.

She had no time to care about those little details women often fussed about. Whether she'd shaved enough or too little. If her naked form would please him, despite the odd stretch mark, cellulite, or scar.

You're perfect, his voice said in her mind, just as his face buried into the soft curls between her legs.

She shook her head and smiled. *No, I'm not. But together we are.*

Erin let out a squeal when Sean tasted her for the first time. He paused and glanced up at her, as though he was asking for permission.

He didn't need to.

Although everything about this moment was well out of her comfort zone, Erin didn't want it to stop. She closed her eyes and surrendered to the moment. To him.

He ran his fingertips up and down the back of her thigh and buttocks. It tickled slightly, giving her delicious goosebumps.

Her already heightened state reached another level when his tongue found her clitoris. Never before had she known pleasure like this. He knew what he wanted. What she wanted. It didn't make sense to separate the two anymore.

They wanted just one thing. To allow their bodies to connect as their minds had done.

Erin took a step back, freeing herself from his grasp. Next thing she knew, she was on her back, and he was on top of her.

"I want you to take me," she whispered.

Her invitation was unnecessary.

I'll love you like you deserve to be loved, Sean thought.

Erin closed her eyes and grabbed a fistful of his hair. *Don't be gentle.*

Sean lowered himself onto her. *Trust me. I'll be everything you need me to be.*

There was no room for doubt. She wrapped her legs around his waist, and placed her hands on his chest.

He wasn't just fit, he was a god. Flawless, like Michelangelo's David. Firm and muscular, with skin so smooth she couldn't resist exploring every inch of him.

Erin cried out when he entered her. She'd been ready

and willing; still, the feeling of his solid manhood filling her to the brim took her breath away.

As he started to move, she remembered the first time she saw him. How he'd carried himself. Confident, deliberate, completely in control of his body. Any of the issues he'd hinted at, about not feeling like he belonged either in the human or shifter world, Erin hadn't seen at all. All she'd known from the start was that he was irresistible.

Now that she knew him better, she could resist him even less.

Capable, powerful, seductive, and kind, all rolled into one.

Her head was spinning, not because of the concussion, but because he was taking her on a roller coaster ride like no other.

Sean played her like an instrument. Speeding up, slowing down, modulating his movements to perfection. It felt so good, so right.

After a lifetime of over-thinking and analyzing everything, Erin's mind was at peace.

There was only room for him. For pleasure. For love.

She dug her fingernails into his back. *Don't stop.*

He didn't. Not until the very end.

Their bodies complemented each other perfectly. Human and shifter. Powerful and fragile.

And their release was earth shattering.

Deep inside, a new feeling start to build. Erin closed

her eyes. All that mattered was the rhythm. In and out. Each time he thrust into her, she moaned into his ear, which only spurred him on further.

He buried his face into the crook of her neck. His kisses gave her goosebumps again, but instead of fighting it, she clung onto him tighter.

Then, it hit her like a freight train. An eruption of ecstasy, passing through her from the inside out. He groaned and pushed into her one last time.

She could feel him. Or he could feel her. They had reached the peak together, then lost control.

Their orgasm sealed the deal. Now they were truly one.

Sean rolled off onto his side and wrapped his arms around her. Erin rested her head against his chest and closed her eyes, waiting for her heartbeat to slow down.

Although she'd never thought so in the past, right at that moment she knew.

EPILOGUE

Sean and the team stood to attention on the front steps of Inverness's small police station.

They were surrounded by reporters. Major Williams was about to give her statement from behind the makeshift podium, just as soon as the local inspector was done introducing her.

The media circus was well underway, but Sean only had eyes for one person in the crowd.

Erin.

His first mission as a fully-fledged Alpha Squad member had turned out very different indeed. He'd hoped to redeem himself after feeling out of his element throughout training. In the process, he'd broken all the rules. He'd conducted an illegal search, he'd involved a person of interest in the investigation, he'd even accidentally ingested evidence that had very nearly killed him.

Teething problems, said Erin's voice in his head. They shared a smile.

She wasn't all wrong. Despite all the challenges, they'd been successful. The squad, together with Erin's unique perspective and support, had stopped a threat more terrifying than anything else they'd ever faced before.

And although he was more aware of how different he

was from the others, he no longer experienced it as a bad thing.

He was unique. Had he been like the other shifters on the team, he'd be dead right now. That exact same mixture of shifter and human DNA which he'd previously seen as a disadvantage had saved his life. And the others didn't care what he was; Eric, Adam, and Cooper had his back and he had theirs.

Somewhere along the way, he'd learned to appreciate what he was.

And he'd even found love.

I'm so glad you're here, he thought, while staring at Erin, who'd positioned herself at the back of the group of reporters and bystanders.

Not as glad as I am.

The longer he looked at her, the more at home he felt. His previous job had been his reason for being, but now, it was her. He walked this earth for her.

The work you do on the squad is important too, you know, she teased.

She was right.

Does that mean you're moving to Wales with me?

Erin shrugged and suppressed a smile.

He didn't need her to answer; in his heart, he already knew. Going forward, they'd be inseparable.

"Well, without further ado, Major Williams from Alpha Squad would like to stay a few words," the police inspector announced.

Major Williams made her way over towards the microphone but stopped in her tracks when a procession of black saloon cars pulled into the square in front of the police station. One by one, the reporters turned around, until nobody was looking at the podium anymore.

A uniformed guard got out of the first car and rushed over to open the door of the second vehicle. Out stepped a familiar face.

A whisper passed through the crowd; soon after, camera flashes started to go off all around.

Who's that, Erin thought.

Sean glanced over at Major Williams. Her expression was tense; clearly she was unhappy about the unexpected intrusion.

That's Oliver Teese, Secretary for Shifter Affairs.

"Here to take credit, no doubt," Cooper mumbled under his breath.

That guy has got to start filtering his thoughts, Sean thought.

Although Cooper's comment was inappropriate, that thought had probably occurred to everyone else on the squad as well.

After shaking a few hands, and posing for a few more pictures, Oliver Teese made it to the front of the crowd.

"Major Williams. Lovely to see you again. I was hoping to say a few words."

The major quickly put on a brave face and stepped aside. "The stage is all yours, Mr. Secretary."

The squad, Sean included, followed Major Williams away from the podium and regrouped off to the left of the crowd of reporters, far enough away to make it clear this wasn't their press conference anymore, yet close enough to see exactly what was happening.

Erin joined them and slipped her hand inside Sean's. *Wonder what he wants.*

"Thank you," Oliver Teese said, before taking his place behind the microphone with a stack of notes. Armed guards flanked him on both sides. "I apologize for the intrusion, but today is a historic day."

Was it?

"Victor Domnall, leader of the controversial anti-shifter group, the Sons of Domnall, has been arrested. In a way, this is the outcome we at the ministry have been working towards ever since he started his campaign of hatred against our new fellow citizens, about a year ago."

Yep, taking credit already.

Erin squeezed Sean's hand. *Perhaps it's not all bad news; let's hear him out.*

"This is not the first time shifters have been targeted, neither will it be the last. What sets this case apart is the sheer scale of the attack they were planning, truly highlighting the cowardice at play here. We are definitely on the right track though." Oliver Teese smiled briefly, before shuffling his papers around in front of him.

"This is why I would like to take this opportunity to

remind the British public that even though Victor Domnall will be awaiting his trial in one of Her Majesty's finest correctional facilities, Alpha Squad is more relevant now than ever. That is why I've championed a brand new bill, which has just been passed by the House of Representatives, which outlines the expansion of Alpha Squad, including an upcoming move into new premises on the outskirts of Cardiff. The land has been allocated already. We'll break ground before autumn."

Oliver Teese went on to outline more improvements and expansions he was pushing for, gaining him enthusiastic applause from the reporters, as well as the local residents who'd turned up to watch the announcements.

Erin had been right; although obviously a publicity stunt on the Secretary's part, him turning up here wasn't all bad. In fact, this wasn't bad at all.

Sean glanced over at Major Williams and Eric, both of whom were doing a terrible job hiding their surprise at the Secretary's announcement. No more dingy old army base. No more playing second fiddle to every other government agency out there. They had arrived.

And despite everything that had happened, or perhaps because of it, Sean was proud to be along for the ride.

Once the excitement resulting from the press conference had died down, Sean and Erin finally got another chance to spend some alone time.

On her insistence that he see at least one of the major sights in the area, they'd gone for a quick drive out of town and ended up at the shores of Loch Ness.

She was born and brought up here, though it had been a while since she'd taken the time to visit. Still, this place wasn't just for the tourists. Its charm remained very real, even to a local like her.

On a cloudy, slightly drizzly summer's day such as today, the loch looked even more magical.

"You were right. It's beautiful," Sean agreed.

Erin smiled.

"It's home," she said.

Sean turned around and gave her a questioning look.

"Up there on that hill, do you see that little cottage there?" Erin asked.

Sean put his arm around her shoulder and followed her gaze. "Yes."

"My late grandmother's house. I used to love visiting her. My mom grew up in that house."

"Is it still in the family?" Sean asked.

Erin shook her head. "No, it was acquired by the Forestry Commission years ago. Something about environmental protection."

"That's too bad."

Erin nodded. She hadn't been back here since her parents passed; too many bittersweet memories. But now, with Sean by her side, she felt ready. She was no longer alone in the world. Plus, she wanted him to know exactly where she came from. What made her tick.

"What about your folks?" Erin asked.

Sean shrugged. "We're not very close."

She had more questions, but this wasn't the time. Now that the case was over, they'd have plenty of time to get to know each other properly.

"We could hike up that hill, if you want," she suggested.

"I'm always up for a hike," he said, kissing the top of her head before offering her his hand.

Erin smiled. Such a gentleman.

They walked in silence at first, though it wasn't awkward or uncomfortable.

With Sean, she didn't need words to feel at home.

Once they'd crossed the road surrounding the loch, and climbed over the barrier closing the track that led right into the forest, she finally spoke up again.

"I know what I want to do now, by the way," Erin announced.

"Oh?" Sean asked, helping her across some fallen tree trunks.

She couldn't get enough of how he looked at her. She felt like she'd drifted around aimlessly, trying to build a career for herself. But until *him,* she'd never felt at home. Not like she used to up at her grandmother's cottage.

"You remember when you first told me about

everything that was going on, and I asked if you had a doctor or someone on the team to brief the local police?" Erin asked.

Sean nodded, and gave her one of those earth-shattering, soul-searching stares.

Erin briefly closed her eyes, trying to fight the goosebumps, but it didn't help.

She took a deep breath, determined to finish what she wanted to say, before he distracted her completely.

"I want to do that. I want to find out all there is to know about shifters. Research those things which until recently no one really knew about. I want to understand."

Erin studied his face.

Sean glanced down at her lips, then made eye contact again. *You're really something. Way too smart for the likes of me.*

Someone's got to do it. Why not me? Erin grinned at him.

I don't know... they say you shouldn't work with your other half.

It seems to work for the major and Eric. Erin winked at him.

You know about that?

Erin tiptoed and wrapped her arms around Sean's neck. *I know everything you know now.*

"It would take a while, though. There's a geneticist at Cardiff University I'd like to study under. Get my PhD first. Hopefully I'll be good enough to join the squad after that."

"You're already better than they deserve."

Sean leaned down for a kiss. If being near him always felt this good, Erin wondered how she would get any work done at all. Perhaps his observation about working with your other half wasn't so silly after all. But they'd make it a success, eventually.

I never thought I'd have this, she thought.

Me neither.

He held her in his arms for what felt like an eternity. She could do nothing but smile.

Then they walked on, hand in hand, right up to the old cottage.

She'd come home.

- THE END -

ABOUT THE AUTHOR

Dear Reader,

Thanks for reading Alpha Squad: Showdown. This is the fourth and final book in the Alpha Squad series, which serves as a spin-off to my well received Scottish Werebears series, which came out in 2015-2016. If you enjoy Vampire Romances as well, you might also want to check out my Vampires of London series in which I currently have three titles out; Alexander's Blood Bride, Michael's Soul Mate and Lucille's Valentine.

I may have only released my first book in 2015, but I'm not new to writing in general. In fact, my mom still tells me to this day about how I would make up stories, and attempt to record them in my clumsy, shaky handwriting from the moment I learned to read and write. From there I went on to write fan fiction and other stuff meant for my own eyes only.

I've always enjoyed stories of the paranormal. Vampires, shape shifters, witches and magic, all featured in the books I loved the most, even when I was still growing up. But it wasn't until much later that I got into romance. One of the first writers (a self-published author just like me!) I came across was Tina Folsom, via her Scanguards Vampire series. I was hooked. From there I went on to read more paranormal romance until I found a new kind of hero I loved: bear shifters, like the kind written by Milly Taiden, Zoe Chant, and T.S. Joyce. What I love about bears is how they can be all strong and independent, a bit reclusive, and almost grumpy, but they always end up having a heart of gold (plus they tend to know their food, and we all know that a man who can cook is doubly sexy). All that (except for the shifting into a powerful bear) almost exactly describes the sort of man I ended up falling for and marrying in real life, so it's no surprise that this is what I started my publishing career with.

To find out more, check:

LoreleiMoone.com (And why not sign up for the newsletter to be the first to find out about new releases.)

You can also get in touch with me via Facebook (search for Lorelei Moone), or email at info@loreleimoone.com

x Lorelei

HAVE YOU MET THE SCOTTISH WEREBEARS?

Before there was Alpha Squad, there were the Scottish Werebears… And if you sign up for Lorelei Moone's mailing list at loreleimoone.com, you get Book 1, Scottish Werebear: An Unexpected Affair absolutely free!

Titles in the Scottish Werebears series include:

An Unexpected Affair

A Dangerous Business

A Forbidden Love

A New Beginning

A Painful Dilemma

A Second Chance

These individual books in the Scottish Werebears series are best read in order. They can also be enjoyed as part of the Scottish Werebear: Complete Collection boxed set.

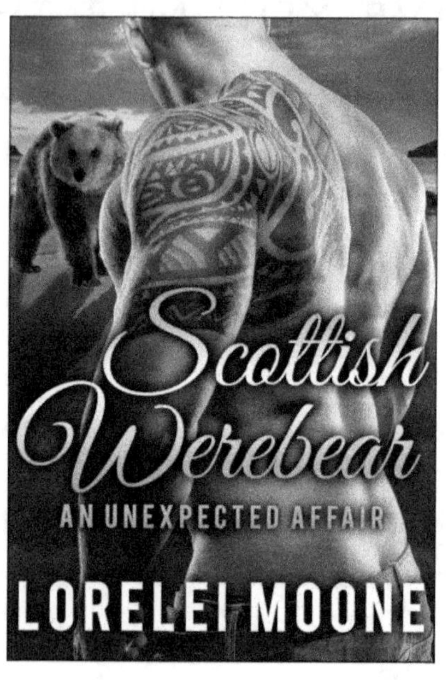

When romance novelist, Clarice Adler, hides herself away in a secluded holiday cottage to finish a book, the last thing she needs is another relationship. Imagine her surprise when she falls head over heels for the man who runs the place. Derek McMillan knows Clarice is his mate, but he's a bear shifter and she's human and the two simply don't mix. They are literally worlds apart; can they find a way to come together?

Get this book for free by joining Lorelei Moone's mailing list at loreleimoone.com!

www.ingramcontent.com/pod-product-compliance
Lightning Source LLC
Chambersburg PA
CBHW071012180726
48291CB00004B/1421